ACROSS
THE
RISEN SEA

Publisher's Note

As I write this, the UK is tentatively emerging from a three month-long 'lockdown', which saw schools and businesses closed and many lives put on hold while others were forced into urgent activity, in an attempt to stem the spread of the Covid-19 coronavirus. This has been a time of enormous anxiety and grief. Millions of people around the world have lost loved ones and had their lives changed irrevocably by this pernicious disease. It has also been a time for reflection, as everything we had taken for granted suddenly stopped. No traffic on the roads and no planes in the sky meant an extraordinary reduction in pollution, leading to clear skies, the regrowth of wildflowers on verges and the re-emergence of birdsong as the soundtrack to our lives in a way it has not been since the Industrial Revolution. Panic-buying and empty supermarket shelves revealed the fragility of our food supply chain and led us to question whether, as a nation, importing something like 50% of our foodstuffs on a 'just in time' basis is a sustainable model for the future.

Confined to their homes, British schoolchildren showed the rest of us how to master communication technology, rather than being mastered by it. Their creativity and kindness led the way in supporting and celebrating key workers, in planting insect-friendly gardens, learning to cook from whatever ingredients were available and re-discovering our bonds with the natural world on permitted outdoor exercise.

This is the third in a sequence of novels from Bren MacDibble based in a climate-changed future world. She has imagined a life with no pollinating insects, in *How to Bee*, and one with no grass-based foodstuffs, in *The Dog Runner*. *Across the Risen Sea* imagines how we might all live should the oceans rise. Once again, her young lead characters demonstrate the creativity and resilience we are all going to need. In wild adventures, Bren's books bravely explore potential future scenarios and offer hope for us all. Just as the UK is now talking about a new 'green' normal, building on what we have rediscovered in lockdown, Bren believes that the next generation 'do not deserve to feel stressed or helpless about the future.'

It has been a privilege and a joy to bring Bren's novels to a UK audience. I hope that her storytelling power and thoughtful optimism will resonate with you and that you enjoy the ride!

June 2020

ACROSS THE RISEN SEA

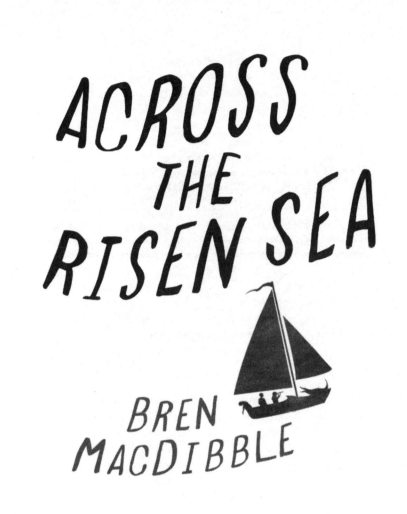

BREN MACDIBBLE

Old Barn Books

AN OLD BARN BOOK
First published in Australia by Allen & Unwin 2020
This edition published in the UK by Old Barn Books Ltd 2020
Copyright © Bren MacDibble 2020

Old Barn Books Ltd
West Sussex

Email: info@oldbarnbooks.com
Web: www.oldbarnbooks.com
Distributed in the UK by Bounce Sales & Marketing Ltd
Sales@bouncemarketing.co.uk

ISBN: 9781910646670
eBook ISBN: 9781910646687

Cover & text design by Joanna Hunt

Printed and bound by CPI Group (UK) Ltd, Croydon, CR0 4YY

First UK edition
1 3 5 7 9 10 8 6 4 2

FSC® helps take care of forests
and the people and wildlife
that call them home.

To everyone trying to live more gently
on this earth. Keep up the good work.

THIS OFF DAY

It's one of them days when everything is off.

A hot sweaty night in Rusty Bus means we kids is all grouchy-tired. Littlies wake up whining and pushing, arguing over whose clothes is whose. Little Margy clings to my shirt tail so hard I can't work her fingers open and have to drag her all the way to the loo with me. Me and my best friend, Jaguar, head to the beach, trying to cool down by taking turns at dipping in the sea pool. Him standing on the sea wall on lookout for crocs, me swimming, then we swap places.

We always do things as a team, him and me.

We's gonna be the best fisherpeople and the best salvagers on the whole of the inland sea one day.

The dawn mist is sitting low, not a gust of wind to blow it or the mozzies away. They's buzzing at my ears whenever I come up for air. I'm slapping at one when Jag sets up whining like a newborn puppy and leaps off the sea wall into the water with me. Splashing and gasping, his eyes wide and wild, he yells, 'Neoma! Run!' He scrambles out onto the beach and takes off, jus' leaving me there! I know he's unnaturally afraid of crocs but this is silly! 'We's meant to be a team!' I yell after him.

His shorts must've been torn on the sea wall, coz all I get in answer is one hilarious pale buttcheek sliding up and down in a corner tear in his shorts as he gallops up the beach.

'Jag!' I shout and scramble out of the sea pool, all splashes and pumping legs up the beach. I turn back once I got a head start on that croc or whatever, coz I wanna know what's got Jag so messy. He's regularly afraid of stuff, but he never up and leaves me to face it alone!

A pale-pink head pokes up above the edge of the sea wall. It's a baby. A tiny baby head, pulling itself up out of the water and onto the sea wall made from old car frames and rocks. I head back down the beach to help it. Who left a baby in the water? Lucky it din't drown!

The baby keeps climbing, revealing more of itself over the rusty metal and rock. It ain't got no hair, and it's unnaturally pink like it got soaked in hot water not cool sea, and then a pair of bright blue eyes is looking at me. There's a tuft of green sea moss stuck on its ear. Its nose is tiny and there's pink flower-bud lips jus' below that. Then its chin shows, and jus' below something that makes me want to scream and run too! Scuttling crab legs! This baby's got crab legs instead of a body!

My heart shoots to thumping flat out, and my feet stagger back from this crawling nightmare, until my bad-sleep head tells me babies can't have crab legs for bodies, but crabs can take anything for shells. It ain't a real baby head, but a doll head. One of them dolls that looks like a real baby. The crab's found it in a drowned house somewhere in the risen sea. It's got its own bit of salvage.

I laugh, which comes out a bit squeaky, and then I whistle up to the littlies. 'Come and be witness to what's jerky-walking along our sea wall happy as can be. A baby-head crab-house!'

Jag comes creeping back down with the other kids, hanging on to his shorts at the back, hopefully coz he's noticed the hole . . . not for any messier reason. All the littlies, even those still hot and sleepy with puffy eyes, laugh and try to be brave even though it's a terrible, terrible sight, that jerky-walking crab baby.

Little Margy wants to chuck rocks at it, but I tell her no. 'Bad enough that crab can't find a decent shellhouse to carry round, now you wanna go and smash the only one it could find?'

We's all there, down on the beach, laughing off our fear, when an aluminium-hulled boat with a bright yellow sun on the prow comes sliding out of the mist.

What a day. Maybe I'm having one of those sweaty sleep dreams that seems so real?

Three tall people, all wearing shiny headbands, is in the boat. They dock, and before the first long leg stretches for the jetty the littlies scatter like scared roos. Me and Jag run and hide too, behind a car-body cottage.

The three strangers hoist large black bags over their shoulders and stride through the village and straight up Cottage Hill like they's the most important thing around. More important than us. More important than our elders even, who come out of their huts and cottages, their silver hair shining in the early morning sun, shouting, 'You there! Whaddya think you're doing here?'

The rest of us, seeing them shiny bands of gold around their heads with a big gold sun on the front, seeing their smooth jet-black hair, seeing their fine clothes, the rest of us is too scared to say a word to them.

Round the back of our island is all cliffs and shores, so full of rocks and driving sea that people don't dare come that way, but our beach is open. With all the car bodies lying round after the risen sea dragged them up here, we took the bendable body-metal and wheels for building and set those solid chassis down as a sea wall, to make anyone come in the front of the bay where we can all see them. There was a time when we'd have people sitting on the sea wall, ready to sound the alarm or see them off, but all our neighbours now is peaceful and we look out for each other, so it's a big shock for us to see people we don't know sailing straight on in like they own the place.

Right away when they reach the top of the hill they pull giant axes from their bags and set to clearing trees and use the wood to mark out big circles, though we tell them not to. The elders tell them we don't cut down the trees, we only take the lower branches, we only take the dead and fallen wood. But they's the biggest people we ever seen. And they go about their strange business like our elders is jus' children, to be yelled at if they get in the way.

Their language is strange and only old Marta understands it, a little. That's how we learn they's siblings from the Valley of the Sun, two sisters and a brother, but we dunno what they's doing on our hill. We don't have anyone who knows their language good enough for that.

Nothing feels right about this day. This day of hot, tired kids, and walking baby heads, this day the siblings from the Valley of the Sun choose to come sliding out of the mist and take down our trees.

EVERYTHING IS
CHANGED

Day by day the siblings from the Valley of the Sun clear the top of the hill, chopping our trees down to huge logs and pushing them into post holes. And we stand by and watch.

'Not so close,' the olds yell at us Rusty Bus kids, when we's daring each other to run in and touch one of them tall siblings. We ain't s'posed to go too close to strangers, all of us kids born and raised here on the Ockery Islands of the inland sea, on account of how strangers can jus' sneeze and spit diseases into the air all around us and we'll come out in festering spots and cough our lungs right out of our chests. The old people say they been to see doctors when they was babies and now they're nokulated and diseases can't get to them. They do the doctoring if anyone's sick, and all us kids who ain't babies and ain't teenagers, we sleep cosy safe in Rusty Bus so no diseases can get to us.

The siblings don't have spots, so we keep at our game of dares. Jaguar says he touched one of the sisters, but I was watching and I think he jus' swiped at her clothes and ran, so I don't believe him. Now when he says he touched one, I poke him hard in the belly to make him jump and stop his exaggerating.

The olds bring the siblings from the Valley of the Sun food each night, coz ain't they queens and stuff? Instead of sitting down to eat and take tea like Ockery Islands people do and let old Marta find out more about what they's doing here, they nod for a thankyou and take the food down to eat, then sleep in their boat.

Each morning, we hope they'll be gone but they're back up and building circles from upright logs. Two small circles and one large one, right on top of our hill. Then they stand a huge pole right in the middle of the largest circle and bring something up in a wooden box from the boat. The whole village follow them to watch.

They take from the box this shiny metal square thing and hoist it onto the top of the tall centre pole. One of the sisters scrambles up after it and nails it there. She casts down wires. Then they dig deep pits in the centre of the two smaller circles and drop metal buckets in there and connect them to those wires from the box.

All of us stand and stare. Marta who can speak their language asks them what it is, but they jus' tell her not to touch any of it or we will die.

Then the siblings from the Valley of the Sun return to their boat and sail away across the inland sea. They've been here four days and three nights and everything is changed.

We all stand and stare at the thing on top of the pole. 'Teknology,' old Marta calls it. 'It must do something,' she says. 'Spy on us, or make it easy for people to find us, or claim us as part of these islands, or help them talk to people way across the risen sea.'

And none of us think this is good. So we wanna take it down and pull down the wood circles, and try to put everything right by moving young trees to this hilltop. But no one moves, and as the earth turns away from the sun and the dark creeps in on us, the Teknology starts up whirring and flashing a red light and we all run screaming back down the hill to our huts and Rusty Bus.

TECH BURNS

Nobody dies that night but all of us are worried. The next day we all push and shove and roll Rusty Bus out of the view of that Teknology, so the little kids won't be up half the night sitting at the windows and crying about the red flashing eye watching them.

Marta says that technology used to do a lot of stuff, but none of it to do with the act of living. She says it was good for spying and talking to people far away and finding your way around, but it wasn't any good for growing food or fishing or building boats or taking care of your own community. She says she's glad we don't have it no more, and can me and Jaguar go and draw the shiny metal box coz she's going to take a boat to the other Ockery Islands and ask them if they know what's going on.

So that's what we do. We got our bit of clean cardboard from Marta's stash and we got a pencil and we sneak back up the hill, brave as anything. Well, I am. Jaguar's pretending he's dropping the pencil so he's got an excuse to fall back. It ain't that he's not brave. It's jus' if that red flashing light is gonna zap anyone, he'd be happier if we found out about it on me first.

Sometimes when we're out salvaging from buildings, Jaguar says, 'Hey, Neoma, can you get across this rusty metal beam?' And that's coz he wants to see how strong it is. You see, Jaguar's real smart, and even if I know for sure he's jus' getting me to test something, he makes me do it anyway by saying stuff like, 'I bet you can't.' I can never turn down a dare. Smart people are more careful. Me, maybe I ain't so smart, coz I like to test things out myself. I'm a doer. I do things.

I'm already circling the pole that holds the shiny metal box by the time Jaguar catches up. I shove the cardboard at him.

'I think we need to draw it like we's looking down on it so we can show how the poles is spaced out in a circle,' I tell him.

Jag nods, so I wrap my arms and legs around a wooden pole on the circle and haul myself up it, using the insides of my bare feet around where the siblings cut branches off to push myself up.

'What you doing?' he asks.

'Getting higher, so I can draw it,' I say.

'They said if you touch anything you'll die!' he says.

'They meant the stuff inside the circle, not our tree poles round the outside,' I say.

'How do you know what they meant?' Jag asks. 'You can't understand their funny speak.'

'Run away if you're so scared. Jus' gimme the cardboard and pencil first.'

Jaguar don't run away, coz he's my friend and he can't jus' leave me here, but what he does do after he passes me up the cardboard and the pencil is stand behind the pole, him maybe thinking it's the square box that might kill him dead.

I sketch out the shape of the square box and circles best I can, hanging on to the top of the pole with one hand and both my feet, then drop the cardboard and pencil down to Jag.

'There,' I say. 'Make that look good with your fancy drawing skills.'

I scramble and jump to the ground and, while Jag is doing some pencil-sucking and thoughtful staring at the square box, I squeeze between the poles of the smaller circle, and use my hands to dig out the loose earth over one of the metal bucket things the siblings buried.

I scrape it out, dirt getting caught under my finger-nails, and soil getting warmer the further I dig down. Then hot in a weird way it shouldn't be.

'Stop it!' Jag shouts when he figures out what I'm doing.

I turn my head to look at him. A waft of sharp burning air smacks my head and I fall back.

'Neo!' Jag screams.

Whatever's down in that hole is sending out burning heat! I kick at the pile of dirt I've made and cover it back over before any more escapes. A stinging burn sets in up the side of my head and gets worse and worse.

'Ow!' I say and turn to Jaguar to ask can he see anything. But he's gone. Jus' a wafting bit of cardboard and a bouncing pencil and a pair of raggy shorts disappearing down the hill, legs pumping like mad.

HOW LUCKY I AM

The stink of something burning hits me then, so I jump up, and tear down the hill after him. I don't go thumping on the hut of the nearest old person like he does, though. I carry right on to the sea. I don't even look for crocs, I jus' plunge straight in, splashing into the water right up to my knees, and stick my whole head under the water. The burning dies down a bit, but the stinging goes on. I take a breath and stick my head under again. Try to feel at it with my fingers. It's lumpy. Blistered, I think. Hair comes out in my hands right off my head.

I stand up in the shallows and yell my head off. I don't wanna be some bald old man!

Marta and my ma come running down the hill with Jag, a whole pile of Rusty Bus kids on their tails, and this is good coz you don't go standing in the shallows yelling round here unless you wanna get et by a croc.

'What you done, child?' Ma asks, which sets me crying.

'Back in the water,' Marta says. 'I think you uncovered a power source!'

I dunno what that means or whether it's good news or bad news to Marta, but I'm pretty sure it's bad news to me. They wash me off and get me up out of the water, wrapped in a towel, and Ma works on my hair with the scissors coz she says some has melted into clumps, while kids crowd round and Marta tells me how lucky I am.

'You're lucky you missed your face,' she says. 'You're lucky you missed your eyes, or you'd be blind. You're lucky your ear didn't melt.'

My ear is real hot so I touch it carefully, trying to make sure it's a proper round ear shape, but Ma bats my hand away.

Finally Ma finishes and sends Jag to get a mirror to show me. He's jus' staring at my scalp when he comes back with it, so I'm guessing it's bad, but I look anyways.

I got a black blistered wide stripe that runs from my eyebrow right up over my ear. And above that, my hair's all choppy. In the centre of the burn there's no hair at all no more. Jus' a bleeding oozing redness under black lumps of blistered skin. No wonder it stings.

'Why's it black like burnt snakeskin?' I ask.

'Coz it's burnt,' Marta says. 'The black will drop off and a scar will form.'

'Yuk!' I say and push the mirror away.

'Did you get a good look at it, before it burnt you?' Marta asks.

I shake my head and frown at her for not being more worried about my head right now.

'Just draw it as best you can,' she tells Jag, and he shrugs at me and heads back up the hill to find the cardboard and pencil he dropped, already dragging his toes in the dirt coz he has to go up there alone.

'I'll go too,' I say and wriggle out of my towel.

'No,' Ma says. 'You need dry clothes and a lie-down.'

'Nah,' I say. 'It's hot enough today to dry me, and my arms and legs work fine!'

Ma rolls her eyes at me, so me and Jag run up the hill and get the cardboard. I watch while he finishes the drawing. My head's still burning like mad. When

Jaguar draws the little circles of poles, above the holes he draws sharp zigzaggy lightning bolts.

I nod. 'That's about right,' I say.

He smiles his most excellent grin at me, which drops away when he sees my head again.

We take the picture we drew back to Marta and then she jus' has more chores for us. Fetch this here, fetch that there, but then she pulls out an old tube of burn cream and squeezes out globs of white cream and smears it on my burns and wraps them up in stretchy bandages and the stinging starts to calm down.

'Come back in the morning,' she says. 'We'll sail to the other Ockery Islands and ask if the siblings visited them too, and if they know what this is.'

'But I wanna go salvaging,' I say. 'Or fishing.'

'No,' she says. 'You need a few days off, until your burn heals over. You can come visiting with me.'

ANGRY
SPOON-STIRRING

The kids in Rusty Bus all sleep good. Everyone's tired out from all that crying last night about the red flashing eye outside, so they're happy it's now jus' a glow behind the trees. Everyone cept me. My head burns. And I can't think how I can get out of sailing from island to island tomorrow, prolly every Ockery Island on the whole inland sea. I wanna be busy salvaging or fishing with Jag. Having fun. Not floating about being good and quiet and polite with Marta.

I think I jus' get to sleep, too tired for the stinging in my scalp to keep me awake a moment more, and then the sun comes peeping in the bus windows and wakes me up. It falls on the sweet round faces of the littlies and sets them squinting and grizzling awake, ruining that sleeping sweetness. Some of them scramble from the bus to get breakfast. The morning breeze floats in the flung-open door, bringing with it the smell of cooking.

What's for breakfast is same as always. A fresh chook egg broken into a hot fish stew. If you eat it quick enough the egg white is soft and the yolk is like runny golden sauce, but if you eat it slow, or stir it too much, it turns to little white strings of rubber in your stew. The littlies like rubber strings but I don't.

Mas and das is coming down to make sure their kids is up and fed and wearing hats and long sleeves, ready to do their chores or have someone to take care of them while they're out fishing or scavenging for the day.

My ma's on her way to go fishing, and comes to the Rusty Bus to feel my forehead and remind me what manners is for when I'm out with Marta. I don't bother saying to her I don't want to go, she'd shut that down real quick. So I tell her my head hurts.

'Of course it does, you numbat,' she says. 'Pain's your body's way of saying don't do that no more.'

'Yeah, but I learned my lesson already, so it can stop now.'

Ma shakes her head. 'For you, my girl, it should prolly hurt you for a whole year to remind you to be safer, but it'll let up soon.' She pulls my flax hat up off my back where it's hanging by its string round my neck, and puts it on my head, easing it down over the bandaged burn. 'Keep the sun off it,' she says and blows me a kiss as she leaves. 'Go gently, child!'

Jaguar's da, Uncle Sorren, is already loading nets into his boat and yelling for Jag to hurry, so Jag does this thing with his mouth where he makes it real wide like a tawny frogmouth and tips his bowl up and swallows down the soup like it's a drink and not chunky at all. I watch his throat stretch with each lump gulped down and when he burps at the end I laugh.

'Your head still smells like a barbecued frog!' he tells me before he fastens his belt of useful tools around his middle, half of them jus' bits of rubbish that might be useful but never is, and gallops down towards the boats clanking like a goat.

'And your burps smell like fish farts!' I yell.

The boats all head out leaving me behind like I'm a little kid, picking through my fish stew with eggs that have curdled to rubbery strings from all my angry spoon-stirring.

NOT DOING STUFF

Marta's collecting things to offer as gifts, teas she's mixed herself, perfumed candles she's made in bamboo pots, salt-dried fish and little egg-cakes with blackberry jam tops. I hope I'm going to get to eat some of those cakes to make up for this boring day.

'Quit your face-pulling, Neoma, it's not like you have to do much today,' Marta says, like not doing stuff is fun. Not doing stuff is the problem! Then she loads up my arms with all her gifts.

When I say, 'Oof!' at the heaviness, she goes, 'You burnt your head. Arms and legs work fine,' and sends me off down to her boat.

Soon we've got her sail hoisted and we're skimming her little tin boat out across the waves, the wind bending out the fabric of the sail. It's a good day to be out fishing, but on the horizon a pile of green clouds with dark edges is clumping like they might head our way. We both stare at them for a while trying to figure out if they's gonna be a problem or not.

Marta was a young woman in the before-times. Before the risen sea drove everyone to the hills. She says she even flew in a plane to visit Old Bangkok and boated along its colourful canals before it was abandoned to the sea. When she was older she visited the great walled city of Sydney after most of it moved to New Armidale. She remembers when clouds were jus' white. She says the green is bacteria and it's the way the earth tries to make things right and clean, and one day, when the earth is done with cleaning, the clouds will all be white as white once more.

Marta's family always lived here in her cottage on the hill. She used to work in the town. I been to Koodah twice when we had surplus dried fish to trade. It's all houses up on stilts and lots of covered boardwalks. The sea's real shallow around Koodah, so they've cut paths through the weeds and mangroves for the boats to come and trade.

I don't like that closed-in feeling. I worry about the crocs. I seen them snatch pigs eating taro on the banks where the creeks come down to the sea and I don't see much difference between a pig on a bank and me on a boat. Jag was the one who pointed that out to me, and it's prolly the one bit of worry that's fully stuck with me.

'Marta, where's the Valley of the Sun, and how come they have a valley that ain't full of water?'

Marta twists her lips to the side. 'North, I reckon. North is where it's warmer, so the valleys be drier.'

The sun is hot, even under my big hat and long-sleeve shirt, and Marta's silently steering her boat so I wet my neck scarf to keep me cool, slide down into the bottom of the boat and rest the not-sore side of my head on the seat. I twist my hat around so it's like my own little house roof on my head protecting my burn, and have a rest.

NEW CLEAR

I don't wake up until the boat is bumping against a jetty and Marta is calling out, 'Hello! Hello, old friend!'

And I'm pretty grouchy about being woken up and that I'm s'posed to be polite and stuff like Ma said right away to these people I don't know, even though they's our inland sea Ockery Islands people.

'Neoma, tie off the boat,' Marta says, and I can do that. I can tie off boats in my sleep.

Old ladies, all before-times ladies, big straw hats and billowy dresses, and chunky beads clicking as they hurry down the jetty towards us, arms wide and full of noisy greetings for Marta, they pull her off the boat, her arms full of gifts for them. Kids and young people and men follow them down to have a look and some move off again, though a couple of men Marta's age hug her too. The men is dressed like Marta and me, long sleeves, baggy trousers, flax or straw hats, coz that keeps the sun off and lets us work. Most of the kids hang around to eavesdrop.

One of the old ladies, with shiny grey curls, looks under my hat and says, 'Ooh!' about the bandage on my head, but turns back to Marta like she don't know if I can talk for myself or not. I guess the bandage makes me look like a bit of a numbat. So I tie off the boat in my neatest knots and trail after Marta as she heads up into the village.

They sit her down at their fireplace and pass around tea. Marta asks what kind of tea and they tell her orange and some kind of bark. Marta looks around like she lost something and then finds me standing there watching and pats the seat beside her, which is jus' a log with a cushion on top. I go and sit and get given a cup of tea too.

'Thank you very much, Aunty,' I say in my best manners. I take a sip. It's not bad, this orangey bark tea.

Marta twists around and looks for the tallest hill, then asks if the siblings from the Valley of the Sun have come here too.

The old ladies say, 'No, what you talking about?' so Marta pulls out our drawing and passes it around and sets to telling the tale of what's been going on in our village since the siblings came.

She stops and asks me to tell what happened when I went poking about.

'Marta gives me and my friend Jag this bit of cardboard and tells us, go up the hill and draw this machine for me. So we go up and draw it from this best angle.' I point to the drawing. 'I'm the doer, so I do the climbing to figure out the angles, and start the drawing off. Jag, he's the artist, so he tidies it up for me, but when he's doing that, I get busy having a closer look at what they buried in the holes, and the dirt got real hot the more I dug, and when I scraped away the last bit of dirt a whoosh of heat blasted my head, knocking me over, so I kicked the dirt and covered it up again before it set fire to the whole place!'

'Oooh!' the ladies squeal. The eavesdropping kids gasp. I'm liking being the one with all the stories here, real well.

'It's a power source, powering the machine,' Marta says. 'But we don't know what the machine does.'

Marta unwinds the bandage on my head and the

ladies say, 'Ooooh!' and 'Oh dear!' and 'Child!' then Marta whispers, 'It might be nuclear.'

I dunno what 'new clear' is but the way the ladies' eyes bulge and they shake their heads makes me think I'm prolly gonna die or something.

'They can't just wander in and put things like that right near your village without your say-so. Don't they respect our wishes to live natural lives out here on the Ockery Islands?' an old uncle says, and the others all nod and agree.

'Arrogant, they were,' Marta says. 'They marched in and started work without so much as a hello! Speaking some Latin language. Have you heard about where the Valley of the Sun people come from?'

The old people all shake their heads again.

'Never heard of them. I did hear of a war up north, and some people setting up a new government. Is it them, do you think?' one aunty asks.

Marta shrugs. 'I couldn't tell you. I can't speak any of those European languages well enough to tell the difference, but if I had to guess, I'd say maybe Spanish? They were tall and well fed, and sailing in small boats so their base can't be far away.'

'But why did they come to you and put something on your hill?' the uncle asks.

'It must do something important if it has a power source,' one old aunty says.

Marta nods slowly. 'Damn technology,' she says. 'We don't need it.'

'And it's right there, messing up your hill!' an aunty says.

'Maybe we can grow a creeper over it,' Marta says.

There's a nervous giggle. Then everyone is back to sipping tea and thinking.

'Where d'ya reckon might be a hill big as our Cottage Hill where maybe they put another machine?' Marta asks, and they explain some place I never heard of called Jacob's Reach. So Marta stands and tells them we'll head there.

I shake their hands and say, 'Go gently!' polite as I can. And nod when they tell me to look after my head.

JACOB'S REACH

Looking down from the boat as we're skimming the waves once more, I complain, 'This is good fishing we're missing.'

'Well then, throw out a line,' Marta says, and nods to under the boat seat. I find a couple of reels and take one to the stern. They've each got shiny silver metal fish on the end with big hooks sticking out their butts. They look jus' like real fish. Marta makes the best lures. Then I'm next best. I been practising with chook feathers that got that same glinting way about them as a fish underwater. Marta has such neat traces too, knots lying flat, and little swivels and weights. I feel kind of important handling them, and her not once saying, 'Be careful with that!'

Soon they're jumping and skipping through the water behind us.

The sun is high and hot, as we sail on towards Jacob's Reach, so I slide into some shade in the bottom of the boat. From under the wide brim of her flax hat, Marta hums some old tune, her watery eyes set on some remembered place out there across the inland sea.

A jerk on my arm wakes me and has me grabbing for the line so quick I get a stitch in my stomach. I grab the handle of the line and set to winding the line back in.

Whatever it is, it's big, and it's hard to turn the handle round and round to get the line in. I do this thing I do where I twist my body, dragging the line across my hip to try and find some slack so I can turn the handle without losing it. Again and again I twist my body dragging it in.

'Reckon it's a big 'un!' Marta says from under her hat. And I'm glad she don't try to help or take over. She knows I can wrestle this fish in, her prolly having wrestled in a few huge fish when she was a girl.

I'm still twisting and winding when the island comes into view and Marta waves to show she's friendly.

From this far out, the top of their hill looks bald, but there's no pole with a box up there. So I wonder if the siblings been here at all.

I'm still twisting and reeling when Marta yells, 'Hello! Hello, old friends!' She drops the sail, and uses the tiller to guide the boat to the jetty.

There's lots of rocks on this shoreline so I gotta land this fish quick or maybe it'll duck down into the rocks and I'll lose it.

People drift down out of the village to the jetty we're fast approaching, with me still in this wrestling match with a huge fish. I won't be letting it go to shake hands and be polite. I don't care if a queen comes wandering down from them shacks. This fish and me got a battle to finish!

These people isn't as excited as the last place to see visitors, but they pull Marta up on the jetty and she's handing out her gifts like it don't matter, and they invite her to sit by their fire. Jacob's Reach people is all dressed the same, which seems real odd. They all wear white shirts and the women have white cotton shawls over their straw hats and tucked into their belts, which looks like a great thing for keeping the sun off but not so useful for getting much done.

There's a boy, the only kid that's come down to the jetty, way bigger than Jaguar, his white shirt dirty grey on the sleeves, laughing at me, twisting and reeling. Ain't no other kids coming down, and I wonder what sort of village it is with no littlies.

'You want some help?' he says, and I'm too shy to tell him, 'Don't you dare!' like I would to Jag.

'She doesn't want help,' Marta says for me. 'Her and this fish got a stubborn match going on, and my money is on the kid.'

Everyone laughs. My face heats up, coz I don't like being laughed at, so I twist hard and launch further into the boat and this big silver fish pops straight up like it jumped, and on its tail, stuck firm, is a baby croc half its size. I pull them both into the boat.

'Neoma!' Marta scolds like I did it on purpose. 'If that baby croc lets go and sets to wailing for its mama, you'll be in a pile of trouble.'

So then I don't know what to do. I got this big fish flopping around at my feet, and any moment that little croc could let go and take one of my toes, so I'm up on a seat, boat rocking, with everyone watching me. I dunno if I should grab that little croc and try to throw him back without getting bit, or unhook the fish and chuck the whole lot back and let the fish sort out his croc problem hisself. And what if the people from the village get upset if I pull the croc off and it wails and draws Mama croc in?

The boy's laughing his head off, like everyone else.

I pick up the line, haul the fish up off the floor. It's almost too heavy for me, specially with that wiggly kicking croc on its tail.

'Can I take the croc?' the boy asks.

I nod and he steps down into the boat, wraps a hand around each little jaw and pries them open. Then he climbs back up to the jetty holding the wiggling croc by its snout and runs on up to the village. I dunno what he's going to do with a baby croc. Ain't meat enough for food, best throw it back and let it grow a little.

Everyone moves on up to the village campfire, and I get busy making sure my fish is proper dead and not gasping and hurting from the hook no more. This fish will feed a lot of people when we get home. Breakfast stew is gonna be super chunky. I'd like to see Jag drink tomorrow's soup. I laugh, and look up. The boy is at a shack talking to a man and holding up the little croc. He points back to me and I wave. But the man don't wave back, he don't even get up from his seat across the door

of a hut with windows covered with old boards. He jus'
grabs the boy by the arm so quick the boy drops the little
croc. Then he sends him off towards another hut.

Weird.

LIVING GENTLE LIVES

Marta is deep into her story about the siblings by the time I walk to the campfire, checking carefully for any snappy little crocs making their way back to the water. Unlike the last stop, people is nodding quietly, ain't none saying, 'How rude!' or 'What's it for?'

When Marta asks, 'Did you see the three siblings?' an old man says, 'They called in here after yours, I reckon. We tells them we don't want no modern tech mussing up our hill and sent them on.'

I'm gonna ask, 'How come your hill's lost some trees then, if the siblings din't stop,' when Marta sees me and waves me to sit next to her.

'Ahh, it's the great croc hunter!' a young man says, and everyone laughs.

'Croc ain't filling at all,' I say and grab one of Marta's cakes on the way to sit beside her.

Marta don't scold me like I think she might, she jus' takes off my bandages to show them my black scar. They all agree with Marta it's a power source, but they don't have a clue what for.

'I'm glad we sent them on their way,' the man says again. 'We don't want our kids getting burnt.'

I look around. I din't think they had kids. Was only that one boy who came down to meet the boat, and I ain't seen none anywhere else. But there they is! Little faces peeping from cracks in shack doors. Little faces peeping from shack windows. And the boy I met, he's chopping wood out back of that hut where he got sent. He looks up and sees me and he's looking back like he's afraid of me now, and he hurries behind the hut like he got stuff to do there.

I'm not feeling good about this place, even if I snagged me one of them great eggy-jam cakes.

I get up to go and talk to the boy.

'Where you going, croc hunter?' the old man says in a way that makes me plop back down in my seat like I did something wrong.

Marta says, 'Not polite, Neoma, to go wandering off when you're visiting.'

'Sorry, Aunty,' I say.

'Did they tell you what the tech does, Jacob, before you sent them away?' Marta asks.

'Not a word,' old Jacob says.

'I couldn't understand them very well,' Marta says. 'What language were they speaking?'

'I dunno. They understood "go away!" well enough though,' he says.

The young man who first called me 'the great croc hunter' sniggers.

'I guess,' Marta says, 'if they have left us with a couple of power sources we could get the electric lighting going in the cottages or maybe the old water heater. Imagine cups of tea without boiling a kettle!'

'You already have too much technology at your joint, what with those solar panels and car batteries you use for cooking and whatnot,' Jacob says.

Marta shrugs. 'There is safe technology, Jacob. It's not all bad. Our electric stovetops cook food for us all without the need to cut down trees, or add woodsmoke to the environment.'

'This is the Ockery Islands. We have an agreement to

leave technology behind!' Jacob says and he frowns so hard, I shrink in my seat and think how lucky I am that the frown is for Marta and not me.

Marta nods, and then shrugs like she don't care at all. 'We each do all we can to live low-impact lives. Our electric stovetops are no worse than your water-drawing windmill there. Let's not lose sight of what really matters here, old friend. Living gentle lives.'

Jacob nods. 'Gentle lives,' he says and lifts his tea.

Marta lifts hers like they've come to an agreement, drinks the last of it and slaps her thighs. 'Well, if they ain't stopped here they've probably stopped further on, and we best be heading that way.'

'Awww,' I say. 'I'm real tired, Marta. Can't we jus' give up this mystery and go pull down our machine and see what happens?'

Marta laughs. 'Yeah, that's probably one way to get to the bottom of this – wait for them to come stomping back asking us questions. You'll be wanting a good sleep in your own bed, I'm guessing. The day has got away from us.'

I jump up. 'Yep!'

SUPER JELLY

We head back down to the jetty and Marta's boat. Behind us old Jacob is having a whispered conversation with the younger man and looking back at us like we're about to be grilled over his campfire for supper. 'Tyrell Weatherman!' Jacob lifts his voice, frustrated. Then he reaches out and slaps the younger man right across the head. The younger man ducks and runs down towards us.

'Can't wait to get home, Marta!' I yell, and run and jump in the boat, getting it untied and holding it for her while she's saying goodbye to all the old ladies.

We take off, and the younger man is already down at the jetty untying a boat too.

'Head for home, Marta, fast as anything!' I say. I twist the sail to catch as much of the wind as I can.

'What's the hurry?' Marta asks.

'Something ain't right,' I say, all hushed.

Then I grin big and wave to the people on the jetty. 'There's a guy following us, and din't you see the top of their hill was part bald on the way in, like the siblings already started here?'

Marta's looking at me, and looking back to the jetty. She gives a smile and a wave. 'Go gently, my friends!' she calls and then turns and hoists a jib to get the wind to really work us along.

No way our headstart will get swallowed up now.

'Maybe he's launching to make sure we're headed home and not onward to ask more questions,' I say.

'These are our people. They don't have any more clue about the siblings than we did,' Marta says.

'Then why they acting so weird?' I ask. 'The siblings were there yesterday, and now they're gone, without setting a machine up or nothing. Why? They din't take no notice of *our* protesting!'

'They got a bad reaction at the jetty and so they left. We need to go on and ask someone else.'

'First we have to make that guy think we're headed home,' I say.

'He's just fishing or something,' Marta says.

I stare back at the boat leaving the jetty behind us. He din't even grab a bait bucket. 'Well, I don't wanna be caught and grilled!'

'Neoma!' Marta complains.

This is the problem with adults. They're too busy thinking they know stuff to see what's going on in front of their faces. If Jag was here, he'd be hanging on my every detail of strange happenings.

'Why'd they lock up their kids, then?' I mumble.

'What?' Marta asks.

'Where were the kids?' I ask.

'Off playing somewhere?' Marta says. 'There was that one boy.'

'That one boy who took the croc and got into trouble for talking to me, and got told to stay home like the rest of the kids, coz they might say something by accident, like littlies do. I seen them peeping down at us sitting round the fire. And did you see when I stood up to go looking for them? And anyway, how'd that old Uncle Jacob know the siblings wanted to install tech on their hill, when he told them no? How did they tell him? You're way smarter and you din't hardly know what the siblings was talking about!' I fold my arms in a huff. I ain't even gonna tell her nothing no more.

Marta nods, frowns. Finally she says, 'Maybe you're right.'

I grin.

'We should head home,' Marta says, and checks the sky and all around. 'Will be dark before we get there.'

'We can't sail in the dark, there'll be tree trunks and bits of old buildings that'll snag our boat!' I say.

Marta looks back at the guy following. 'We'll see how far we get.'

The guy falls further behind coz we're going flat out, tacking to catch the best wind. But we're taking a pretty direct path home, and the guy maybe figures he ain't never gonna catch up to us, so he swings about and heads back to his village.

Once he's out of sight we sail into the marshes and tie up to a good tree branch to sleep. Marta gives me cakes for dinner, which my stomach is super happy about, and we wrap in blankets in the bottom of the boat. Me with a fishing knife in my hand on account of the crocs that might live here and jump on me while I'm sleeping.

It should only take a couple of hours to get to our

island when the earth turns back towards the sun and shows us a safe path, so we'll have fish stew for breakfast at home. I'll have to wake Jag to show him the fish I caught, before we add it to the stew. He's gonna be super jelly about that and cakes for dinner!

SMELLS FISHY

I lie watching the stars and listen to the water bumping
the boat, worrying about why my head still hurts, and
worrying about what that guy would've done if he caught
up to us, and next thing I know I'm waking up and
Marta's already got us sailing again.

'Come on, sleepyhead,' she says. 'We gotta tack.'

I check the sea all around and I can't see that guy's
little boat. Way in the distance is a bigger fishing boat
stopped and already fishing. I release one rope and haul
in the other rope as Marta tacks, and soon enough Cottage
Hill is on the horizon with its fully bald top of the hill
and that little flashing red light. Rusty Bus is sitting there

in the middle of all the shacks, its blue and white paint shining like it's got no rust at all, and the breakfast stew already steaming in front of it.

We dock and I grab the fish and run up through the village. It's my ma's turn to make breakfast, so I run and give her a hug and show her the fish I caught, and tell her the tale of the croc. Then I hurry up the steps of Rusty Bus and slide that fish in beside sleeping Jag, right under his nose.

He stirs, he groans, he screws up his nose, he jumps up and bangs his head on the bunk above him. He grabs his head with one hand at the same time as he sees the fish and gasps and shoves it away. The spines jab his hand, so he pulls it back quick. Then he looks at me, standing there laughing, and his terrified eyes go narrow. 'Neo!' he yells.

'Look how big it is!' I say. 'My biggest catch yet!' I say. 'And when I hauled it in there was a croc hanging onto its tail!'

Jag don't even know what face to make now. He looks at the fish like he's impressed and wants to hear the story of the croc, then he looks at me and says, 'But why's it in my bed?'

I laugh. 'Jus' be glad I got the croc off first!' I yell, and grab the fish and run back out to Ma. Together we cut it up and add it to the stewpot. Everyone's going to be eating fine this morning.

Ma says she's going salvaging, and that's my absolute favourite thing, and then she strokes my hair and says, 'You should be resting this damaged noggin today.'

I say, 'No! I'm coming. This scalp is practically healed! And the sea water will do it good!'

Ma sighs like she knows I'm pretending but I can go anyway, and I run to tell Jag to hurry up and get his lazy butt out of his fishy-stink bed.

We eat breakfast as fast as we can, with those big chunks of fish, and some of the adults even have second helpings, then we run down to the boats to get ready.

Jag has his belt with the useful stuff swinging from it, and he's sniffing his shirtfront. 'I smell like a fish!' he says and gives me a push.

I push him back. 'That's better than you smelled yesterday!' I say.

I'M A SEABIRD

We head out on Ma's favourite boat, *Licorice Stix*. Two small black hulls with a strong net slung between them, great for hauling back stuff we need, and behind that a little deck area with an actual ship's wheel for steering. We hoist the sail and Ma takes over steering and chatting to her friend Dizzy while me and Jaguar go and stretch out on the net under the shade of the sail. It's a couple of hours across the inland sea to where the sunken city lies on the old surf coast.

We lie on our stomachs, watching the water skim along under us. Ma hoists the jib and we move even faster, so fast that my dangling arms is wet from the spray coming off the hulls and my fingers slap a stinging wave every now and then. I stick my face right through a net square and pretend I'm a seabird flying and skimming over the waves looking for fish to dive on.

Jag says a shark once came up from the sea below and nudged him right in the butt through this net, but I've never seen a shark do that. Jag is unnaturally afraid of sharks. Like there's a regular fear of sharks that will make you careful, and then there's Jag-level screaming if a bit of seaweed touches his leg fear of sharks. Crocs too. Jag's afraid of going in the water, even though he likes swimming in the pool on our beach as much as me.

Jag asks me all about the croc on the end of the fish, so I tell him the story of how I caught it, and then how I pulled it in in front of a whole village, and Marta told me off for hauling a croc into her boat, so then I have to tell him about the boy who took it for me, so then I have to tell him about how all the kids in the village were hiding, and that makes me tell him how strange the villagers were acting, and that makes me tell him about the guy that followed us out to make sure we'd finished our snooping around.

'Neoma!' Ma calls. 'Don't you be telling stories about our Ockery Islands neighbours!'

'It's all true, Ma You can ask Marta. We's prolly lucky to be alive!'

'I will be asking Marta. Now pick a building to head to, something that might have some good salvage.'

On the horizon is the tall buildings of the old surf coast, now flooded by the risen sea.

Jag sits up and swings his arm around straight out like it's a magic finder of things and yells, 'That one!' He's pointing at the Ocean Tower.

'Went there last month,' Aunty Dizzy says.

'The Silver Water!' I say. It's shorter, but the tall buildings get too many salvagers.

'Silver Water it is!' Ma says and heads *Licorice* that way.

Most of the surf coast din't get moved out of like the areas around it, coz they had a big sea wall. The surf coast was where the rich people lived, pretending they was safe from the flooding that was washing out the poorer coastal towns and making salty swamps of farmland. But Cyclone Summer sent six cyclones nose to tail and destroyed it. Survivors moved inland to a mountain range same as the poor people. But the sea rose so quick they din't get to take everything they owned. Then when they were camping out on the ranges in tents bad diseases came and most of them got sick, so they wasn't able to come back and clear out their stuff anyway.

My ma was there, and when my da got sick, he stole a little rubber boat and put Ma in it, and me, jus' a baby, and told Ma to row inland as far as she could. She rowed for three days and then found Marta's cottage on the hill and people who would help her. She says it was the seagulls picking through the rubbish that made everyone in the mountain refugee camp sick, and there weren't enough drugs in all the world to kill the new kind of sickness the seagulls brought. We're very careful with rubbish now. Never leave anything out the seagulls might come down for. My da said he would follow us when he got better. Ma left the little rubber boat tied to a treetop next to the sea wall for three months, she says, but he never did come. Or maybe he came looking and went right past. One day, she left me with Marta and sailed back to the ranges to look for him. She never tells me what she found, but I think what she saw that day makes her think he died.

If I was a seabird for real, I could skim over to those mountains and have me a good old look around and maybe understand what it was that made her give up on Da ever coming to find us.

MY LUCKY FLOOR

We head over to the Silver Water. At sea level the windows is smashed in. They's all been punched in by the waves and those sudden storms that come whipping up from out at sea. It's eleven years since Cyclone Summer, long enough for the sea to pull the ground out from under the towers on the other side and set them tilting and crumbling, but not so long that you can't still find something worth getting from the safe towers on this side. Most of these buildings been picked over anyway, specially the lower floors. But if they've only been picked over by a few people in small boats, maybe there's still stuff for us.

Ma pulls *Licorice* in close to the Silver Water and Dizzy throws a grappling hook right up two floors. There's no point searching where the storm tide can reach. Those floors been swept through by big waves a billion times.

'Off you go, little monkeys,' Dizzy says.

We grab our sacks and scramble up the rope. Each sack has three floats tied to it. I go first, of course, in case something's gonna go wrong. Jag wants to make sure it's safe.

I wrap my hands around the rope up high on a knot, then pull hard and haul my feet up and wrap them around the top of another knot. I used to get sore stomach muscles and sore arm muscles, and sore fingers and sore insides of my feet, from hauling and pushing on these rough knots, but now I practise every day and my muscles are strong and my skin is tough. I get to the window, already smashed in, and pull myself over the sill, avoiding the sharp bits of glass.

'Go, Jag!' I yell.

Jag scrambles up the same way, but when he gets to the windowsill he pulls out a little hammer from his tool belt of useful things and smashes the sharp glass out of the way before he climbs over.

'Remember! Canned food!' Ma yells, like she thinks someone might've left stacks of canned food somewhere.

'Come on,' I say to Jag and tiptoe through the glass and across the room. Things are damp, green with mould, drowned by storm waves, ain't nothing here for us. I lead him to the stairs and up and up, flight after flight.

'This one?' Jag asks, kicking at a half-falling-down door.

'Nup, someone's been here already. We're going to the top,' I say.

'What? Nah, Neo, it's too far!'

I laugh. 'That's what everyone else already been here said!' I keep on climbing. I climb till my thighs ache, concrete step after concrete step, this part of the building only ever meant for emergencies back when they had something called lifts to pull people up and down I climb till Jag is way behind and yelling at me. Then I see writing that ain't jus' numbers on the wall, promising me something more than jus' somewhere where people used to live. This isn't the top but it will do.

'Here!' I yell down to Jag, who comes grouching up the stairs, his tool belt clanging as it swings from side to side with every slow step. Each step he takes with his hands pushing down on his knees, like his thigh muscles gave up a few floors ago.

I hold the door open for him, and he grumbles through and holds on to a wall with barely any mould on it.

'Why?' he whines.

'Coz this is my lucky floor,' I tell him.

There's no numbered doors here, jus' glass doors either side of the hall. I run to the nearest and push them. They don't move. 'Jag! It's locked! We're the first!'

'Really?' Jag asks. He runs over like his legs don't hurt no more and says, 'Stand back!'

I don't, coz I'm here to do stuff, not stand back.

He pulls a little thing with a red handle from a pouch on his belt, and then his hammer. Then he slides himself back along the wall so jus' his arms is sticking out over the glass. 'Get back!' he says again.

I take two steps back.

He uncovers a super sharp point on the red thing, lines it up on the glass, and pounds it hard with his hammer.

There's a huge bang like an explosion and then Jag is pulling his arms in, squeezing his eyes shut and turning away from the door as it clouds and explodes into glass chunks that throw themselves onto the floor in a tumbling mound and slide outwards, striking my bare feet and sending me hopping a few more steps back, landing on the glass-chunks and hurting my feet more.

'I tol' ya!' he says, then throws his sack down on the crumbled glass in the doorway. 'After you!' he says.

The sack does hardly anything to make the glass not stab into the soles of my feet, shooting jolts up my legs, curling my toes, but they ain't sharp enough to cut the skin. I lay my sack down too, and Jag follows after.

Then I grab up my sack, pick my way through the scattered chunks and run. It's a room full of chairs and tables and amazing paintings on the walls and one side is all grimy sea-streaked glass. Ma tol' me that in the times before the risen sea, people would come to places like this and sit down and people would jus' bring them food. I can't believe people used to live like this. Imagine food brought right to you while you sit on your bum like a newborn bub!

SILVER WATER

I push through some big double doors and I'm in a room with everything built from shiny steel. There's a rack with all kinds of glass jars with lots of different coloured herbs and spices and pots and pans on every shelf and giant spoons hanging from hooks, and knives, sharper than any Jag's got on his belt. I turn to tell him, but he ain't behind me no more. I push through to a room to one side of the steel kitchen and there's dozens of packets and cans and giant white bags with mould creeping up the sides. The cans are rusty round the tops, the labels faded and hanging off them. I shove some of them into my sack. Cans like Ma said. She's gonna be so happy.

'Jag!' I call.

His feet pound on the tiles behind me and I spin to show him the amazing find of a whole small room full of food.

'Come see the sky!' he says first. His face is weird-stiff.

I drop my sack with a clunk and follow him running back through all the tables and chairs to where he's pushed one of the grimy sliding glass doors open a bit. I squeeze out, follow him between tipped and rusting chairs and tables to the edge of the balcony, and even before he cries out anything, that smeary cone of runny black and green cloud in the distance makes my mouth go dry. Lightning flashes, cracking through the black clouds, kicking out at the sea like it's taking giant jagged white-legged steps towards us.

'If we fill our sacks, we can jump,' I say, not wanting for our find to be lost to other salvagers before we get back here.

'We can't jump from this high!' Jag says, and starts towards the door.

I grab his sack from him. 'Then you take the stairs, I'll jump.'

'Neo! No! We'll come back!' Jag's voice is squeaky.

'It's food for summer when it's hard to grow stuff. It'll

keep us all fed. I can do it.'

Jag looks at me and looks at the door, and I can tell he'll choose me. He'll make me jump first but still he won't leave me to do this alone.

'Listen,' I say and grab his shirt. 'I need you to run down the steps fast as you can, and tell Ma about the storm and to bring *Licorice* around to this side of the building for me. Can you do that?'

Jag nods. 'I c-can,' he says, like he's surprised to be given a safer job to do. He presses a rope from his belt into my hands. 'Don't jump more than ten floors, you'll break your legs off.' He takes off.

I drag his sack through the kitchen, slide more cans off shelves into it. I throw a solid-looking pan and a ladle into my bag as well. These sacks are super heavy and once they're all tied off I can't hardly drag them to the balcony. I'm hoping three floats each will keep them afloat long enough for Ma and Dizzy to get hooks to them.

Then I tie Jag's rope to the railing of the balcony. I'm gonna get down a few floors before I jump, like Jag said. He's the voice that I'm missing in my own head sometimes. The voice that keeps me safe.

The storm's kicking up white tips out on the sea, boiling up the clouds and making them swirl dark and angry, full of hate for the little land creatures that dare to be out on the edge of the wide risen sea.

Ma said they din't used to have sudden storms rolling around all the time when she was my age. She said they came on with the risen sea and the heat in a way no one could've guessed.

'Neoma!' Ma screams below, coming around the building in *Licorice*. Jag must've slid down railings to get to them that fast.

I heave the first sack up to the rusty rail and balance it there, cans on either side, then the second. 'Get your hooks ready!' I yell.

'Leave them!' Ma yells. 'We have to go!'

I hear her fine but pretend I don't coz I worked hard for this salvage. I push the first sack over and it goes down so fast and slaps the water so hard, I think I must've dented all the cans. It sinks immediately, the floats dragged down after it, down into the dark choppy water. Then a hint of yellow as the floats pull up, looking for the surface they jus' can't reach. Dizzy's dangling from a stanchion, hooking the ropes with her long hook pole and pulling it in. Yay!

I climb over the balcony rail and give Dizzy a moment before I pull the other sack over, let it fall past me, down and down. I move my hands to the rope, stick my bum out and try to walk down the wall, feeding the rope out as I go. It's rough on my hands and my arm muscles burn. Then my feet hit nothing on the next balcony and I'm jus' swinging hand under hand, fingers and shoulders tight and burning now too, grappling at the rope with my bare feet, trying to spread the weight. I'm thinking we went up twenty floors above the water, but there's no way I'll last doing another ten like Jag wants.

'Hold on!' Jag yells at jus' the right time.

I do. I hold on for two more floors, hands slipping, muscles weak. Then two more, blisters burning on my hands. My shoulder joints scream at me to stop, let go. But still I hang on and get one more floor down. My blisters tear and I want to be in the cold choppy sea to stop the burning more than anything. So even though I've only scaled down six floors, I push my feet against the wall, push out and let go. The air roars like it wants to tear my ears off. My shirt's flapping like it's already torn. My shoulders is suddenly good again and I wish I hadn't let go so soon. I clamp my knees together, pull them up like I'm kneeling for them to bash a hole in the surface of the water, and link my fingers behind my neck, with my elbows hard together in front of my face. I take a deep breath.

Then *blam!* My shins and ankles sting and my knees is shoved up, smacking my chest, my elbows ripped up and apart, my fingers drag my knuckles over each other as they tear apart, water pushes up my nose and tears at my hair, pulls on my sore burnt scalp, and I sink like a rock. I kick against the water, heavy and pulling me down. My ankles complain like the fronts of them got sprained a bit, but they ain't broke like Jag said. And soon, I'm kicking for the surface and Jag is in the water there, holding on to the hook with one hand, his head under the water, hair all fanned out floating around his head, eyes round and blinking and cheeks puffed out like he's some kinda puffy-cheeked angel. He reaches a hand out towards me and I take it, let him pull me up through the surface into the empty air and the waiting hands of Ma. She drags me into the net of *Licorice Stix*, the net knots scraping my skin like I'm a wet-skinned eel that she drug up from the deep.

'You alright, kiddo?' she asks.

My mouth opening to answer only brings the water from up my nose out the back of my throat and sets me coughing. Water splutters from my mouth, pours from my nose. I nod.

'Good haul,' she says, and runs to help Aunty Dizzy get *Licorice* up to speed.

TROUBLE?

The storm's pushing the wind ahead of it and we're riding that sticky wet wind. My clothes flap but don't get any drier as we're driven inland so fast *Licorice Stix* is tipping up on one hull, and a good thing too coz the waves driving in behind us is big enough to swamp the net. Me and Jag scramble back and over the tall side of the platform between the two hulls, to ride clinging to the seats with Aunty Dizzy while Ma works the wheel.

The sky gets unnaturally dark as we go skudding past the old hills. I figure we don't need to take shelter there, we can make it all the way home to where it's safe from storms and from people who might find our boat or our canned food to their liking and take it from us.

'Tacking!' Ma screams and we all duck as the boom swings across to the other side of the boat. Jag leaps on the winch to tighten it off, and we change seats to the high side of the boat as she tips up the other way.

There's a small boat in the channel, being hit from the side by the waves pushing in ahead of the storm. It slides sideways, rocking wildly, and gets dropped by every wave.

On a fine day we'd stop and investigate, maybe take it back to its moorings if it's got a name on it we recognise. This one looks real familiar. And I can't think why, until it spins a bit towards us and a golden sun on the prow reflects a flash of lightning.

'Ma!' I yell over the crashing waves. 'It's the siblings' boat from the Valley of the Sun!'

'Din't they tie it off proper?' Jag asks.

'Something's happened to them,' I say. I know it, deep in my heart. I've known it since I went to Jacob's Reach.

'I ain't stopping to tie it on, Neoma, no matter what's happened,' Ma says. She's frowning over her shoulder but not at me, at that swirl of green and black chasing us down. 'Storm's almost on us.'

'Sail close,' I say. 'I'll grapple it, and we'll tow it in.' This boat could have clues about why it's bashing around out here empty without a sibling to be seen.

'You'll break the grapple rope before you get it up to the same speed we're going,' Ma says.

'I'll winch it out, so it don't!' I say and nod at Jag to get ready to do that for me.

'Okay, but likely we'll have to cut the rope anyway if it slows us down.'

Ma sails close and I hand the end of the grappling rope to Jag to let out as needed, and wrap it round the winch. Last thing I wanna be doing right now is handling rope. My hands is raw meat.

Then I lean way over the keel, holding on to a stanchion real tight, swing and drop the grapple hook gently, without too much sliding through my hand, into the boat and drag it forward to hook it onto the board across the top of the prow as we sail on by.

'Okay!' I yell to Jag. 'Let the rope out so it turns and gets up to speed.'

I go to turn away but something pale twitches in the bottom of the siblings' boat, and I wonder if a fish got slopped in there by a big wave, but the pale thing has a thick ribbed tail, and in a flash of lightning it becomes a hand, palm upwards! Someone's in there, under the tarp!

I scramble back to the deck. 'Someone's in there!' I yell.

Ma looks at me like I grew an extra head. 'Don't lose that rope, Jaggy-boy!' she yells, dropping the sail a little to slow *Licorice* so we don't lose our tow, then turns to Dizzy. 'What kind of trouble are we hooked into right now?'

BENCHTOP SKIN

The storm blows us on, throws waves at our backs, each wave sloshing a little more water and foam into the boat behind us, so I reckon whoever's in there's prolly gonna drown, if the boat don't sink before we get to our bay.

Soon the rain joins the waves sloshing at us and the lightning kicks and stomps all around the sea beside us, kicking up the waves like it's mad at us for stealing that boat from it.

The Valley of the Sun boat picks up a little speed, so Ma hoists the sail on *Licorice* again, but we don't seem to get moving any faster.

'It's slowing us down!' Ma yells. 'We might have to cut her loose.'

'No!' I say. Imagine that. Imagine the sea stealing this mystery from us. Imagine going my whole life wondering if I really saw a hand or a fish down there in the bottom of the boat. So we keep pushing through the storm, relying on the Ockery Islands around us to keep the smashing waves down. *Licorice* creaks as she's torn two ways, pushed on by the punches of wind in her sail and held back by the siblings' boat.

Cottage Hill's jus' ahead, with Rusty Bus halfway down the hill already tied down tight with tarps, and the scattering of huts around it, all of it sitting in the long yellow grass made bright by the earth turning away from the sun, the lower half of the sky dark from the storm, the upper sky pale pink. In that weird early evening light, home looks to me like a shiny perfect place. I can't wait to get in there, turn into the bay, tie up *Licorice* safe, and find out what's going on in the siblings' boat.

But when we drop sail and dock, Ma tells me to run for Marta if my legs still work after what I've put them through. Jag she tells to tie off *Licorice Stix* with lots of bumpers, hard against the jetty, then tie down the sails.

I run for Marta's cottage. 'Marta! Come quick!' I yell. My ankles really do hurt when I run that hard.

Marta comes out to the porch of her cottage. The porch's got extra ropes tying it down, and she stands, hanging on to one like the wind and rain will blow her away.

'It's the siblings' boat!' I yell. 'We found it drifting, and someone's in it!'

Marta don't even grab a raincoat when she hears, she jus' tucks down her head and runs through the stinging rain towards the jetty. I chase after her, but when I get there, Ma yells, 'You help Jag tie down *Licky Stix* and go get dry in Rusty Bus. We don't know if these siblings got some disease!'

'Ma!' I yell, coz ain't I the one who knows about the mystery at Jacob's Reach? Ain't I the one who went with Marta to try to find out what's up with these siblings and their machinery? I gotta be here to find out clues.

'Neoma! I will tell you anything I find out!' Ma yells like she knows that I gotta find stuff out. 'Now help Jag or get to Rusty Bus and try to fix up whatever bruises and blisters you did to yourself today!'

'Ma!' I say, but she's right.

I can't hardly tie things down on *Licorice* properly in the driving rain with my blistered hands, but I keep starting knots and calling Jag over to finish tightening them for me. Anything to stay near the jetty to see what happens.

They haul in the siblings' boat and tie it off with bumpers hard against the other side of the jetty. All our fishing boats is already tied out in the bay to permanent anchors where they can rise and fall with the sea and swing about without hitting each other. Much safer than being anywhere near land, with the waves smashing in. Even our little dinghies is pulled high up above the tide line, almost to the shacks and tied down.

Marta's in the boat as soon as it's tied, shoving under the tarp, shouting things that the wind and rain drown out, then she has Ma and Dizzy dragging one of the siblings, one of the women, up onto the jetty by her arms and the three of them grab limbs and run with her up to Marta's cottage.

Me and Jag ditch the ropes we're pretending to tie, even though every bit of *Licorice Stix* is already tied down, and scramble across the jetty to look into the boat. Lying in the bottom of the boat is the other sister sibling, her eyes open and staring up at the tarp roof.

She's pale like I never seen. Skin of patchy marble like those benchtops in the apartment buildings of the sunken surf coast. It's like she's made of rock, not flesh no more.

Jag pulls me back. 'She's dead!' he shouts. His eyes is so round and his face so white the truth of it hits me like a cold-handed slap to the face.

I look once more on her marble skin, and this time the sight of her dead and crooked sets my heart pounding and my sore scalp tingling. 'Stone-cold dead,' I whisper.

Both of us run screaming through the wind and stinging rain all the way to Rusty Bus.

ONE SIBLING LEFT

It's no disease that puts bruises on a woman's face and breaks her ankle and leaves her for dead in a boat, I know that for sure, but Marta and Ma ain't telling me that one of our neighbours did this coz the sibling herself can't remember, one of them blows to her head making her forget everything. She forgot so much that even two days later when the clouds had dried away, the sun burning us once more, and she was well enough to sit up, it was hard to make her believe it was her sister wrapped in the shroud we were setting to burn on the funeral pyre.

She wanted us to unwrap her face so she could see for sure, but Marta said no one should go looking on faces that've soaked in sea water, not if they want to remember that person as they once were.

'Stone-cold dead,' I whisper to the sibling even though she don't speak our language, and take her hand so she won't feel so alone. Me beside her chair, her not even able to stand to honour her dead sister. She looks up at me, maybe sees my bandaged head, matching her bandaged ankle, and maybe thinks we're a little bit the same, her and me. I wanna tell her I lost a da too, way before I was old enough to remember him, but now's not the time even if she could understand me.

She squeezes my hand as the flames leap higher and heat billows out at us. Squeezes it real hard and both our hands get slippery with sweat.

Marta speaks of the dead sibling, about how strong and tall she was, and how she came to work and did her work single-mindedly, whatever it was for, we wish we knew, and how she never deserved this unknown fate. Marta says the sibling left alive is called Gerra, and that it is hard to be the surviving sibling with no siblings left. And it's the after-times, so we all know that the old people lost family in the rising sea and the diseases, and homeless wars afterwards. So we understand the tears rolling down their tanned and wrinkled faces. We lost family ourselves, me and Jag, even though we was too small to remember them.

Then Marta offers Gerra the crown with the sun on that her sister wore, and chicken soup with canned creamed corn. There's nothing like a good tasty soup to fill the hole in your stomach, which is real close to the hole in your heart that you get when someone dies. We all watch her eat it, watch the tears streaming down her face, watch each mouthful bulge and slide down her throat like it was dry lumps of flour, her never once sobbing for her sister, not even sobbing about her leg which must be aching so bad. Then people carry her back in a sturdy chair to Marta's cottage to rest.

'What do you think happened to the brother?' I ask Jag.

'Prolly et by sharks,' he says, coz that'd be the worst thing Jag can think of, him being so terrified of sharks.

BUD OF AN IDEA

Marta calls a meeting, adults only, and they have it all
squeezed into Ma's shack coz Marta has Gerra recovering
in hers. Even though it's adults only, me and Jag sit
outside with our backs to the wall under the window.
Ma says it's clear the siblings met with 'foul play' and
whoever did the 'foul play' was hoping the siblings' boat
would be taken out to sea, them not knowing it might
wash back in a freak storm. Them not knowing a sibling
was still alive. So now the 'foul play' evidence was sitting
here on our shore, we're in trouble. Coz if the people
from the Valley of the Sun come looking, it's gonna look
bad, and if the people that did the 'foul play' find out

about Gerra still being alive, they might have 'unfinished business'.

I've no clue why adults speak to adults and still speak in code words like 'foul play' and 'unfinished business'. I dunno what's wrong with speaking plain and saying what's on your mind.

Jag's da says he could run the siblings' boat up a secret creek and hide it good in the bushes. Marta says that can't be done soon enough, and maybe Gerra will be well and leave on it one day soon, and tell the people from the Valley of the Sun how good we were to her, then all our problems will be over. In the meantime, if they come looking for the siblings, it'd be easy to find out that this was the last place they worked on account of the transmitting device on our hill. We'd be 'prime suspects' in 'foul play' with Gerra, not able to say for sure it wasn't us that killed her sister, her only having seen us giving her a funeral and not remembering anything of the event.

'And the way people gossip in these islands,' Marta says. 'Who's to say no one saw *Licorice Stix* towing home the Valley of the Sun boat or saw it tied to our jetty during the storm, even though it's been tarped-over since then. By now it could be back to everyone that we found the boat at least. We have to keep a lid on the fact that Gerra survived.'

'It was dark and grey,' Dizzy says. 'We could say it was jus' a fishing boat that someone came and claimed a couple of days later, someone from the Whaleback Ranges. It got swept inland. People from our islands don't know many from the Whalebacks.'

'Good,' Marta says. 'That's our story. A fishing boat from the Whalebacks. You hear that good and proper, Neoma and Jaguar?'

We pop our heads up into the window and say, 'Yes sir, Aunty Marta!'

'And if people from the Valley of the Sun come looking?' Ma asks.

'We'll have to hope Gerra remembers who did do this to her, or trusts us enough that she'd never suspect us of hurting her family,' Marta says, and sighs.

An idea starts then, a little bud of an idea that flowers in my head the more I think about it. Part One, disconnect that box so it don't kick out light or a signal or look like the siblings stopped here at all. I'm the only one who can do it, coz I know it don't kill you, it jus' burns you. Part Two, stick to Gerra like a tick, make sure she understands we're good people who don't do bad things. That way she'll tell her people we couldn't have been the ones who killed her sister.

PART ONE

Part One's easy. Dizzy's sleeping in the front of Rusty Bus, on duty in case any of the littlies wake in the night. She opens her eyes as I sneak down the steps.

'I gotta piddle,' I whisper.

'Urrr,' she groans, and goes back to sleep. Me not being a little kid, it's jus' annoying for her to be waking up to make sure I'm okay. I'm almost too big to live in Rusty Bus. My feet is already hanging off the end of the bus seats we kids use as beds. If me and Jag weren't so useful keeping an eye on the littlies I reckon we'd already be living in shacks with our parents.

The moon is full, outlining our whole village in

shadows I know like I know my ma's face. First I go to the stoves and put on the two big pot-mitts that live there. I been real hard on my hands lately and I don't wanna burn them on top of my blisters and rope burn. Then I head up the hill, picking a toe-stubbing way over the debris the siblings left when they wrecked the trees on our hilltop, easy to see in the flashes of red light. The night is warm and muggy. One of those after-storm nights when you wake up five times and move to a cooler bit in your bed anyway, so I figure I ain't losing sleep. Halfway through shimmying up the pole to the red-light-flashing machine I wish I'd thought to put pot-mitts on my feet too, them still sore from rope burn and bruised from chunk-glass.

I grab the wire feeding from that scalp-burning energy source and yank it hard out of the machine, and drop it to the ground. The world goes from a strong red-flashing light to a weak red-flashing light that only lights as far as the poles. I shimmy around to the other side and yank down the other wire from the other power source, and that makes no difference at all to the weak red-flashing light.

I dunno how it still goes with no power source, but maybe it dies slow like a fish outta water when no one is kind enough to put a knife through its brain and stop its hurting.

I stumble down the hill, drop the pot-mitts next to the stove and hurry back to my bed in Rusty Bus.

PART TWO

The next morning when the horizon turns back towards the sun, it's hard to tell if the red light is even working it's so weak.

When I tell Ma I don't wanna go fishing, I wanna go help Marta with Gerra, she squints her eyes real hard and says, 'Whassup, Missy? One day you would rather go fishing than spend a minute with Marta, the next you're turning down fishing to hang out with her?'

'Well, I jus' figured out it ain't so bad hanging out with Marta, after you made me do it,' I say.

Ma shakes her head. 'I don't reckon you can get

into trouble with Marta looking out for you, so it's all good, as long as she wants you there.'

So then I have to do this thing where I have to go talk to Marta and come back and talk to Ma, and then go back to Marta. So I take two bowls of steaming fish soup with eggs up to Marta's cottage. I dunno if they like their eggs runny or hard, but if they're gonna have any choice, I gotta run fast before the eggs set. I'm concentrating so hard on keeping the bowls from slopping that I almost run into Gerra as Marta is helping her out to a chair in the sunshine. I stand back and wait till she's settled in the chair, then hand her the soup, giving her my friendliest and most trustworthy grin. Then I fetch a stool and a blanket for her to rest her leg up on if it's throbbing like your toe does sometimes if you stub it hard. That throbbing gets less if you put it up in the air.

A few weeks ago I had to hop all the way up from the beach coz I stubbed my toe and it hurt to put it down. I guess I'm lucky my burnt head is at the top of my body.

Marta says right away she'd be pleased for the help, and thanks for the soup, so then I run back down to eat my own breakfast with much runnier egg and tell Ma what Marta said in the exact words Marta used so she knows I ain't lying to jus' play games all day or something.

'Get Marta to put some burn cream on your head while you're there,' Ma says.

'What you doing?' Jaguar whispers.

'Taking care of Gerra so she don't think we was the ones what killed her sister,' I say.

'That's stupid,' Jag says. 'No one can prove something that din't happen, and taking care of someone who can't even speak to you is boring.'

'Won't hurt to make sure,' I say.

'But you'll miss fishing, you know you love fishing, and how we gonna be the best fishing team on the inland sea if you's always staying behind?'

I smile. 'Give you a chance to catch a fish as big as mine. Don't forget to catch a croc too!'

'Ha! You din't bring back no croc, though, did you?'

I give Jag a shove and wait with the littlies waving as the fishing boats head out, then make sure they start their chores with the letting out of chooks and collecting eggs and sweeping out Rusty Bus and such before I head over to Marta's. I put Dizzy's little daughter Margy in charge. Margy's every bit as bossy as Dizzy if you give her a chance.

LIKE A TICK

Marta says that the swelling's gone down on Gerra's ankle so now we gotta put it in a solid bandage to keep it from moving while it heals up. First we have to clean and oil the skin and then wrap it in the softest cotton.

So she has me with a pan of warm water trying to wash the most painful part of Gerra's leg and I don't dare hurt her the least bit coz I'm trying to get her trust. But I'm a doer, and my hands is still rough and blistered from too much doing, and I wish it was someone more gentle than me taking on this job.

'You're gonna have to work faster than that,' Marta says when she sees me wiping tiny gentle strokes down Gerra's shin. Gerra's looking on and hasn't flinched once.

'I gotta be careful. Hasn't she been through enough?' I ask.

'I was hoping to get to a few other jobs today,' Marta says.

But I don't speed up. I wipe away dirt and salt water whiteness gentle as I can, then I spread on oil that smells like flowers, and makes the fine hairs of her leg shimmer in the sunlight, then I wrap the softest cotton carefully, around and around.

'More around the ankle and foot,' Marta calls. 'We don't want no bones rubbing on the cast.'

Then Marta moves in with packets of something that she managed to salvage from some hospital by the looks, and starts soaking lengths of bandages in a bowl and wrapping them around and around Marta's foot and right up to her shin. She works fast and a bit rough and still Gerra does not flinch or moan. Staunch!

The bandages set hard as Marta works, and she smooths the outside, and goes to wash up before her hands set hard and white too.

While she's washing, I sneak into her house and fetch Gerra a cup of that special rice wine Marta keeps in a big jar on her table. I hold my finger to my lips when I give it to her, so she knows it's a secret.

Gerra don't take it. She jus' stares at me with hard dark eyes, and my stomach turns. I've made a mistake. I'm s'posed to be making her trust me and now, jus' by trying to be extra kind, I've proved myself a thief!

I duck back into Marta's cottage and pour the rice wine back into the jar, leaving the door open so that Gerra can see me do it, if she cares to turn her head. She don't. And I'm thinking that she could be a bit more kind to me after I was so careful cleaning her leg, and don't she know I'm the one who hooked her boat to be towed back?

I'm standing next to Gerra trying to be good, when Marta comes back.

'Why are you standing there looking like a possum stole yer apple?' Marta asks.

'I'm jus' sad for Gerra losing her sister,' I say.

'Well it's probably for the best she don't remember it happening,' Marta says.

'But what if she remembers half of it, and what if she gets it muddled and the Valley of the Sun come here with a war to kill the ones who killed their royalty?' I ask.

'The siblings weren't royalty,' Marta says. 'They all get a sun crown when they turn eighteen, Gerra told me.'

'But how do you know she jus' din't say that, so that we don't panic about having royalty here when all this trouble is happening and try to hide it, like Jacob tried to hide them ever being there?'

'Neoma! You just accused Gerra of lying, us of being capable of deceit and Jacob of worse, in one sentence!'

I did! There's no way I should be around Gerra. Nobody trusts someone who don't trust them! I try to play it down. 'I'm jus' s'posing,' I say.

'Well, words is dangerous. We need to keep Gerra a secret until we can help her get home, and any rumours that she's even here could get out of control, real quick.'

I nod. I been seen stealing, and now I get told off in front of Gerra, even though she can't speak the language, a telling-off is a telling-off. 'I think I should go check on the little kids, help them do their chores,' I say.

Marta nods.

'Tell Gerra that's what I'm gonna do,' I say, coz I wanna look like I'm good and useful. Ma always says you can be stupid and grumpy, but if you're useful you're worth your weight in gold.

Marta speaks that strange language and Gerra lifts

a hand and waves. This is the best response I got for all my efforts, so I grin, and wave and take off. So much for being on her like a tick. I should maybe jus' stay away before I ruin everything.

SINKHOLE!

Jag comes back with a huge fish, long and golden with a golden tail, but I gotta pretend like it ain't as good as the one I slapped him with, so I try to play it down.

'S'okay,' I say.

'It's fatter, not longer!' he says. 'So it's got more meat, and that's important, coz that's what we eat.'

'Yeah, maybe,' I say.

'You ain't even trying to argue!' he says, all huffy.

So I tell him how I tried to be a tick on Gerra and stuffed up.

'You should prolly leave it to kids who's better at it.'

'What d'ya mean?'

'I mean, you always doing sneaky stuff, and even when you go away with Marta, you come back with stories about crocs and kids hiding and strange villagers.'

I shove him. 'All that happens to be real,' I say. 'I don't make up stories, it's jus' I'm normally dragging you around with me, so you know it's true!'

He laughs like he's happy he finally got an argument.

'Anyway,' I say. 'If you and me snagging her boat and hauling it in isn't trustworthy, I don't know what is.'

'That's why you got nothing to worry about,' Jag says. 'Coz we ain't done nothing wrong.'

And I wonder if I should tell him what I got up to last night, pulling the wires out of the tech thing. But I don't, and if I ain't telling Jag, my best buddy, I ain't telling no one.

Up the hill, the red light is completely out. Gerra is sitting out in front of Marta's cottage still, in the shade. If you din't know where to look you wouldn't see her. I wave to her but she don't wave back. Why would she?

There's a splosh sound, a chunky splash behind us. Jag hears it too, coz he grabs my arm. And then there's a scream. I spin and take off running towards it. 'Bring a rope!' I yell to Jag.

Little Margy's screaming. Margy's slipping and sliding on her back, her chooks running squawking, from the sinkhole opening up in the ground in front of the chook shed. The ground under Margy is crumbling away, great cracks forming around a bubbling muddy hole, and those chunks are sliding away into the frothing water.

'Margy!' I scream and run straight at that sinkhole. Sinkholes, always opening up and stealing people. It's not gonna take one of my littlies. I run flat out. Jag is the only one fast as me. He'll be off that jetty with the rope and right behind me. Him and me, we're a team. I don't even have to waste time looking back.

I'm about to jump to where Margy is scrambling to pull herself out of the mud, but the edge falls away under my feet and I drop and slide into the cold boiling water. It sucks at me and pulls me under, drags my arm one way, my legs another, and I'm kicking and pushing against chunks of land. I'm shoved back up by a rush of water. Margy's going down. I reach out, snag her shirt, haul her to me, find her grabbing arm under the water, but it's slippery with mud so I use her hair, pull her back to the surface. Coughing, gasping, her eyes blinking wild, mud streaming down her face. Me treading water, kicking hard as I can at chunks that scrape my bare legs, everything churning, boiling and sucking. I kick like I'm fighting. I pull her head close to my shoulder. She's kicking like mad too.

The mud sucks my legs, twists them, grinds a hunk of something at me, pulls me down again. 'Take a breath!' I tell Margy. I been teaching her to swim, but I don't know how long we're going down for. It's hard jus' keeping a hand on her in all this pounding muddy water. I twist my hand in her shirt so it's wrapped around good, so I can't let go. Mud pushes grit in my eyes. A hunk of land hits me square in the back as it falls in, blobbing around, breaking up, and it pushes us sideways. I kick, push up through a surface of slopping mud and grass, pull Margy up with me, both of us spluttering.

'Jag!' I yell.

A rope plops beside me. I wrap it around my arm. Jag pulls, and I pull at Margy and we're dragged through the churning mud, gently first, then the olds arrive in a panic of yelling and we're torn across the surface of that sinkhole so my arms burn like they're gonna rip off. My elbows graze, and I spit mud and grass from my teeth coz we hit the crumbling edge. Me stretched between the rope and Margy, like I'm a hunk of chain. I can't do nothing to protect my head from the crumbling bank.

Then people grab me and Margy, stand us up and yell things. I scrape the mud from my eyes and I'm face to face with Ma yelling about what did I think I was doing.

'Jag was right behind me!' I yell back. 'We's a team!'

Then she's squishing me against her chest even covered in mud like I am. Her heart thumps in my ear super-fast like it's gonna bust through her chest. Then Aunty Dizzy is there, wailing and hugging Margy and me and Jag all at the same time, Jag squirming away coz he don't wanna get covered in mud.

Margy and me look like swamp creatures, cept Margy has two clean lines under her eyes, where she's been crying. I go to wipe away the tears and smear mud across her cheeks. She grins. A pop of white teeth in a mud-brown face. I hate to think of her maybe drowned in all that mud. I'm glad me and Jag was close.

Aunty Dizzy takes me and Margy off for a shower and clean clothes, leading us right past Marta's cottage where Marta calls, 'Great work, Neoma!' and Gerra lifts her hand and waves. Ha! Finally she's seen me do good!

A NEW PLAN

The next day I'm back fishing with Jag and his da, Uncle Sorren. I've asked the littlies to bring things up to show Aunty Gerra, like their favourite chook or the biggest egg, or if any interesting fish or salvage come back on the boats today. Like Jag said, maybe they'll be better than me at convincing her we're good. This is where I wanna be, out fishing.

We're pulling out of our bay in *Licorice Stix* when Jag's da says, 'You know what I noticed last night? I noticed that red light not flashing.' He rubs his fingertips through his beard, making a scratchy sound. He turns and looks right at me, making me suck in my breath and think for excuses. Then he says, 'I reckon maybe they turned it off. I sure am glad about that. Not natural, that flashing light.'

I look back at the hill, and nod. 'Reckon so,' I say and rub my chin too.

We live simply coz our folks learned that what people do can damage the planet. We have our shared electric stovetops, our boats only use sails or little solar motors, our lamps is solar rechargeable or have little crank handles, and luckily for us, before the risen sea came flooding in, there was already enough fabrics, and clothes, and things like pots and plates, chairs and beds, to keep the world going for a very long time, so we don't even need to take down any of our trees. We salvage anything we need.

There's still people living in cities, the people who could afford to move to high ground when the cities relocated. Most of them way south of here, away from the endless heat. But most of our folks were pushed from their homes by flooding and hunger, and they couldn't afford to be more than beggars in the cities. They don't ever want to live in a way where they could get that hungry or in danger of getting sick again, so now we live off the sea.

Jag's da, Sorren, lost two small sons, and he and his

wife fled here but she was still too weak when she had Jag, and died anyway. Jag was born here and fed by some of the mothers in the village, including my ma who was nursing me. He's a true child of the village, his da says, and he don't ever wanna live anywhere where small boys get thin and sick and die while rich people get fat.

'Weird thing that light,' Sorren says. 'I hope Marta can figure out what it's all about.'

'Makes me angry, the way they put it there without our saying so,' Jag says.

Jag's da sighs. 'Anger is hardly ever useful, son.'

We sail out to our favourite fishing spot and I hook two tiddlers that I apologise to and throw back before Uncle Sorren hooks a keeper. Jag hooks a keeper too, but it's a female full of eggs so we put her back too, or we'll have no fish to feed Jag's da when he's old and grey.

We try another spot, and haul in four more large fish, then we pack up. Five large fish can easy feed twenty people and two other fishing boats went out today, so we don't need anymore.

We're done real quick so I ask, 'Can we go see Jacob's Reach?' I tell Jag's da that I think I can get to the bottom of the mystery of what happened to the siblings if I talk to the kids there.

'It's too dangerous, Neoma,' he says. 'Coz what if you're right?'

'You believe me?' I ask him.

'I don't know for sure,' he says.

'Drop me off and I'll walk around the back of the village. I jus' wanna check out their hilltop, see if there's any starting of a circle there. If we know Jacob is lying, we'll know he's covering up,' I say.

'Yeah, Da,' Jag says. 'Coz what if the Valley of the Sun people come and blame us? Shouldn't we know for sure whether we can send them on to look at Jacob's Reach?'

'You kids!' Uncle Sorren says like we's nagging him. 'I been worrying about the same thing. I saw how it was when the sea rose and the governments retreated to the cities, saying if you want any protection move to the slums. They turned their backs on the upcountry folk, them not set up to manage a spread of islands and mountain ranges, and not able to feed the city as it was. The people that stepped in to try and control the thieving after they left were no better than thieves themselves, their laws made up and changing on a whim, so they could line their own pockets. I'm worried that if we don't know what happened to Gerra and her siblings, we'll be blamed.' He swings *Licorice Stix* about. 'We'll drop you off, Neoma, you go up the back of the hill, stay out of sight, jus' to check the hilltop. Not to talk to anyone. We'll go to the jetty for a visit, offer them a couple of fish as gifts to keep their eyes busy, and we'll catch a couple more on the way home to replace them.'

'Good plan,' I say, grinning coz I can't believe I got an adult to agree to this! Uncle Sorren is real nice.

GIVEAWAY FISH

'Don't anybody mention the siblings or Gerra no matter what. I'll answer those questions if they come up,' Uncle Sorren says.

I nod. They drop me around the back of the island Jacob's Reach village sits on, and head back out to sea, to come in again to the jetty. I duck down behind some driftwood and check the place out. The beach is empty, the hills and trees above all quiet.

I run up the tideline and into the scrub, and pick a path through to the forest. I run a few steps and stop behind a tree and look around, then run a few more, the way I seen lizards run. Moving things is easier to spot than perfectly still things. The trees here have been sawn and axed more than ours, so the forest is open. On Cottage Hill we take branches for building but not much else. Jacob's people burn them in campfires and stuff, so I can't see how they won't eventually clear this hillside. Marta's right. They could live a bit more gently if they used some of our solar and batteries. The batteries and stuff was jus' lying round anyway.

Finally I get to the top of the hill. There ain't no circles of wood, but the way the land's cleared in a big circle makes it look like they might have started. My foot goes down into some soft earth. A post hole, filled in, maybe? I take a step around in a circle and stomp my feet again. Another soft patch. No doubt about it, the siblings was here.

There's a pile of cut logs as if it's firewood drying. Behind the pile of logs there are some trees with things carved into them. And a stump with a firewood log sitting on it. I creep closer. There's zigzaggy lines carved into the firewood log, made by a knife while the tree was alive. It tried to heal over those cuts a year or more ago, I'd say.

There's a foot-scuffing noise, and I duck back into the trees. It's the boy who took my croc. He was the only one in the village happy to see me and Marta, even if he laughed at me.

He's walking head down, staring at the trail, so he hasn't seen me, then he kneels in front of a tree with two corners cut into it, each one like the letter L. He pats the dirt under the tree and speaks to it quietly, then lifts his head and talks to the tree. 'Well, Lucy Loo,' he says. 'I got my butt kicked for losing that rope, and kicked again for tearing my shirt in trying to get it back. Now look!' He waves his hands at the tree and his sleeves unroll and flap about over his hands. 'Now I gotta wear hand-me-downs from Tyrell Weatherman!'

I know who that is. That's the guy who chased me and Marta halfway home.

The boy who helped me with the croc looks at the stump with the log on it. The one carved with the zigzaggy lines like the letters M and W. 'No offence, Aunty. This here's a good Tyrell-sized shirt, but it's gonna be wore out before it fits me.'

He settles down with his legs crossed and goes back to mumbling at the ground.

I tiptoe closer and stand behind him. He's pretending the ground is someone that needs updating on the news. He's talking about fishing and food, and his da and someone who ain't learned to play fair at footy yet.

'What you doing?' I ask.

He twists about. 'How long have you been there?' he asks.

'Jus' got here this second,' I say, coz it's prolly embarrassing to get caught talking to the ground.

'I'm talking to my cousin, Lucy,' he says. 'She's buried here.'

'Oh,' I say. I heard about burying people in the before-times, but with the rising sea and sinkholes, we generally burn the dead. It's about the only time we have a fire. 'Sorry about your cousin.' I sit down cross-legged next to him and pat the ground like he did.

'It was a while ago. But she liked to talk, so sometimes I come and talk to her,' he says, and shrugs.

'That's nice,' I say. 'She prolly gets lonely on this big old hill all alone.'

The boy waves his hands around at the other trees with things carved on them. 'She ain't alone. Uncle Silas is over there, and Grandma up there, and right here next to her is Aunty Meryn.' He waves at a patch of ground in front of the stump.

'Oh, so the things carved on them is the names of people?' I ask.

'Why're you here, anyway?' The boy frowns.

I wave back the way I came like it's not important at all. 'We followed a school of fish around the back of your island and saw some massive crabs, so Uncle Sorren dropped me off to do some crabbing there and said he'd take some spare fish around to your jetty to pay for the crabs while I was catching them, but he was so long gone I climbed the hill to see where he was. I best get back down there, in case he's coming for me.'

'You can see the village from jus' down there,' the boy says and points back down the trail.

'Crab pots to collect,' I say. My brain is saying, *do what Uncle Sorren said, don't mention the siblings*, but my mouth wants to do something to help the other part of my brain that wants to know what happened. And coz I'm a doer, not a thinker, it blurts out. 'Hey, when those Valley of the Sun people came, did something happen?'

The boy's face goes pale and he stands up. 'I ain't s'posed to talk about them,' he says. He turns and stomps on down the hill. Then he stops and turns back. He waves at the marked trees. 'But if it was your mother . . .' He shakes his head. 'We din't mean for the women to fall on the rocks. We ain't killers.' The boy puts his head down and runs.

'Whose mother?' I ask. But he's gone.

I turn and run the other way flat out, back down the hill to where *Licorice* is sailing into view, coz what if he tells Jacob I'm here? Will my crab pot story hold up if I din't bring no crab pots?

WHAT'S HAPPENING?

I'm on the bank bouncing with the news, then run out onto the mud of the beach and let Jag's da grab my arm and swing me aboard without even stopping.

'They's hiding something, for sure!' I say, all puffed and breathing heavy from the downhill run. 'The siblings was on top of the hill, coz there's post holes been covered over and logs been cut and cleaned.'

If I tell the rest about meeting croc-boy and what he said . . . I'll have to tell how I asked the question I was told not to ask, and Uncle Sorren won't trust me to go off alone and do stuff ever again.

Uncle Sorren shakes his head. 'Now we know,' he

says and sighs, and we head for home, throwing a couple of lines out to replace our giveaway fish as we go.

When Cottage Hill's in sight, Uncle Sorren jumps up and shades his eyes. I see it too. The red light is flashing again. I dunno how. I pulled those wires good. But he ain't looking at that, coz he says, 'I thought I hid that boat good.'

The Valley of the Sun boat is docked at our jetty again, gold sun glinting on the prow.

'Did it float loose?' I ask.

'Not the way I dragged it out of the water and tied it,' he says.

There's no one down on the jetty when we tie off. The other fishing boats is not back yet.

There's shouting up at Marta's cottage and little round faces peeping out from trees and out from under Rusty Bus. The littlies is hiding. There's strangers in the village! The Valley of the Sun boat is full of provisions, and different coloured tarps to what I was specting. 'This isn't the same boat!' I yell to Uncle Sorren.

'You kids take *Licorice Stix* up creek and hide!' he says, and takes off running up the hill to Marta's cottage.

Me and Jag look at each other, loose off the ropes, push *Licorice* off from the jetty, get her little solar motor whirring to back up and swing the boom to catch the wind. We tie her up jus' out of sight up the creek mouth and take off back towards the village. No way we're gonna hide as well. We're gonna find out what's happening.

IT WAS ME!

Two tall men from the Valley of the Sun stand in front of some of our people, long dark hair held down by gold sun crowns, and they have guns, actual guns! They're holding them up to Uncle Sorren and the other Cottage Hill people, like they're saying *don't get any closer.*

Marta's speaking flat out in the strange language with Gerra and another woman from the Valley of the Sun. This woman is much older but still her hair is black and straight, not all grey and frizzy like the elders of our village.

'What's happening?' Uncle Sorren calls.

'They think we were hiding Gerra here,' she says. 'Coz we hid her boat and someone's pulled the wires on their machine.'

'Tell them I can bring her boat, we only hid it for her safety,' he says.

'I told them already. I told them we've done nothing but rescue and care for her, and she's told them we've been kind,' Marta says and throws up her hands. 'But her siblings are dead or missing and someone's pulled the wires from the machine, and that makes it look like we's covering up.'

'Tell them about Jacob's village,' I say, and Marta frowns at me hard, and my ma grabs my arm.

'We do not spread rumours,' Marta says to me with her lips real straight.

I nod.

'Go look after the kids,' Ma whispers and pushes me away.

'Who here would pull the wires after seeing Neoma's head?' Marta asks the Cottage Hill people. 'Whoever it was will have to own up and explain why, so it will stop looking like we tried to cover something up.'

The adults all look at each other, and nobody answers. I could go away like I was told to. Jus' walk away like Jag's already started to. But I don't and he stops, waiting for me.

The woman with the black hair that should be grey speaks again, and Marta holds up her hands and tries to calm her down. Even Gerra tries to make her stop.

Marta's face goes real pale. 'She says we were told not to touch it or we would die. She says it is an offence to touch their equipment and whoever did it must be punished. And if no one comes forward she will punish me for letting it happen.'

All the adults shout at once how it's not our law, we never wanted that stuff on our hill, and it's unfair. The men with the guns yell and wave them around, but no one is quietening down.

'It was me!' I yell. *'It was me!'* I scream. *'I DID IT!'*

THE OTHER CRIME

Everyone stops yelling and all eyes stop on me.

I shrink. My stomach sucks in and I feel like I'll shrink right down until jus' the soles of my feet is left standing here, stuck, in the dirt.

'Why?' my mother asks, and her eyes is dark like the thunderheads that boil up over the sea sometimes. And I'm afraid to answer in case lightning kicks out from her eyes.

'Why?' Marta asks.

'Coz I wanted to give Gerra time to get to know us and see we could never do bad things like the things that happened that she can't remember happening.

And if nobody knew the siblings had been here, then maybe they wouldn't look here first.'

Marta tries to explain it. And one of the men with guns steps forward to grab me, but first Jag grabs me and pulls me behind himself, and I think *good, I can get a head start, that lanky giant won't be able to keep up if I run into the trees.*

But then Jag says, 'No! It was me. I was angry that they put up something dangerous without even our say-so, and it burnt my friend.' He rips my hat off and points to the hairless burn across my scalp.

'That ain't true!' I yell, but the man grabs Jag anyway. Why'd he have to go and say that?

Jag's da runs and jumps on the man's back, wrapping his strong fisherman arms around his throat. 'Let him go! He's jus' a kid!' he yells.

'Stop it!' I yell. 'It was me!'

Marta yells so loud I swear she jus' broke her throat. It's a wail like a night-screecher, eyes more desperate than I ever seen.

Everyone stops and looks at her. Uncle Sorren slides to the ground. Puts his arms at his side like he been told off.

The old woman with the black hair speaks our language and says, 'Someone must answer to our law, someone must pay. We will take the father.'

'No!' everyone yells.

'It was me!' I say.

'No,' Jag says. 'It was me. I'll go.'

I punch him in the arm. 'This ain't a game!'

'Ow!' he says, like it is.

'We don't answer to your law,' Marta says, standing as tall as she can to look the old woman in the eyes. 'We are not part of your land.'

'You are. You just don't know it because you don't keep in touch with the outside world. All these abandoned islands have been claimed by the Valley of the Sun. If you defy our laws then you will be at war with us, is that what you want?'

Marta shakes her head slowly. 'If this is true, then no decent society punishes children.'

'We hold the father accountable, but the child has admitted his crime and given proof of motive. And he can work off the father's debt. Leaving you with a fisherman here to feed you until he does.'

'No!' Jag's da says again.

'We will return the boy when he has worked off the

debt,' the old woman says. 'As to the other crime . . .'

One tall man scoops up Gerra and carries her down to the boat, the other grabs Jag's arm and drags him away. 'No!' I shout. 'I did it! Jag would never go near that stuff. It was me! Take me!'

Jag's da sets off after Jag, and the older woman pulls a gun from her robe and fires at him. I duck as something leaves the gun, flies through the air and stabs into his back.

He grunts, reaches for it, arms twisting behind snatching up his back, as I'm scrambling in the dirt to get to him, to help him. He drops to his knees, flops forward, and I get there jus' in time to catch his head and slow its fall to the ground. I wail, coz he's dead!

The older woman steps over me, pulls the thing from his back. 'He'll sleep for a day or two but he'll be fine,' she says, and leans down to my ear. 'Do not touch our equipment again!'

I gasp. 'You know it was me! Let Jag go! Take me!'

'Ha!' she says. 'A wild spark like you will be no end of trouble. Think long and hard about this lesson, child. You might learn something.'

She turns back to the rest of the adults. 'As to the other crime, we will find who attacked our people and they will be punished far worse than this. Think long and hard about who it might have been or we will take another from this village to pay the debt of our two lost people.'

Everyone cries out, 'No!'

THE BRAVEST

I chase Jag down to the boat.

'Is my da okay?' he asks, blinking through tears.

I jog along beside him as the tall gold-crowned man, hauls him along. 'Yes, she says he's jus' asleep. It was a little dart thing.'

'Oh,' Jag says, and takes a deep breath.

'They know it was me,' I tell him. 'They know it, but they're taking you anyway! Why did you have to say it was you?'

'Coz,' Jag says. 'You's my friend.'

The man pushes me away at the jetty, and yells at Jag and points to the Valley of the Sun boat.

'Jag, I'm sorry!' I yell, as Jag gets in the boat. 'Jump in the water and swim for it! Then they'll have to take me!'

Jag looks at the water, but of course, he's afraid of crocs. He won't be jumping in.

The old woman comes down to the boat, talking quietly to Marta. Marta still trying to strike a deal, first in their language, then in ours. 'He's a good boy,' she says. 'He's a good fisherman. His father's already lost a wife and two boys, you gotta bring him back to us. He's a good boy.'

The old woman says she will. 'But people need to understand not to touch the equipment. Our security is at stake. There are wars going on over the remaining land that you people of the inner islands don't understand.'

'We understand now,' Marta says. 'Don't take our boy. He's a child of this village more than any other child, born of a dead mother and raised by all the mothers.'

The woman jus' turns and looks at me and tilts her head, like I'm the one who caused all this. But I was only trying to make things right with Gerra.

I stand there on the rocky shore, the sun burning shame into my bare, burnt scalp, burning right down to the soles of my stone-pricked feet. 'I'm sorry,' I say.

The boat pushes off and sails with Jag clinging to the stern staring back at me with wide, sad eyes, back at our village, back at that red-flashing light, and now I'm glad it's flashing so he'll see it way out at sea. Way out there, he'll look back at the land disappearing on the horizon, and he'll see that light so he knows where we is for longer.

Marta turns and looks at me.

'I'm sorry,' I say and I've never been more sorry about anything ever, and I want her to say something to make me feel bad, or hit me or hug me so I can cry.

She puts a hand on my shoulder, and gets her face low and level with mine. 'Child,' she says, and sighs like she's emptying her heavy heart. 'I knew you was up to something. You should've told me.' Then she turns me around to face the village. Ma is sitting with Jag's da's head in her lap. She looks up at me with eyes dark and damp, lips pulled tight so I can tell she's gonna let me chew on this misery and wrongdoing for a while before she talks to me about it.

The kids come out of the trees and crawl out from under the bus. The other adults rush and hug them like they were in danger of being taken too. Some adults is jus' standing, watching our Jag sail away. 'Don't listen to her. You're not wild,' Marta says, her voice tired but kind.

'Could you maybe put in a good word for me with Ma?' I whisper.

'She'll calm down,' she says. 'You're brave. The bravest of us. Don't lose that.'

But looking at the village now, their hearts all broken for Jag, I don't know if jus' being brave is enough no more.

UNDER THE
MOONLIGHT

Everyone's sitting around teapots on the stove this evening of losing Jag, trying to talk each other through what happened and how they'll calm Uncle Sorren when he wakes. No kids have gone to Rusty Bus, they's jus' trying to burn off their fear of what happened by playing tiggy under the moonlight where they can scream and scare themselves, safe from Valley of the Sun people who might steal them away.

I been avoiding people. Can't stand the looks, coz they all know it was me that got Jag into trouble. So no one notices when I sneak down to the creek with a bag of supplies, untie *Licorice Stix*, and push her out into the bay.

I'm going to get Jag back.

FIND JAG

I ain't sure where the Valley of the Sun is other than north, but I don't think they'll sail overnight much past the old surf coast. They'll stop somewhere, they'll light a campfire to cook whatever fish they've caught, and I'll see a fire on a shore where there wouldn't normally be one, and I'll follow them. I'll wait for my chance.

Licorice Stix has black sails, so I don't have to worry about anyone seeing her. There's jus' enough light from the moon for me to haul the sail. What I can't see is the white woolies on the sail that tell me which way the wind is coming from, so I ain't moving very fast. Which is a good thing. The channel out to sea is pretty much swept clean by the tide, but I'm using the dark land outlines in the moonlight and my memory of having sailed that way so many times to avoid rocks and other sticking-out dangers.

The night air is fresh and damp, and the waves slop at *Licorice's* hulls.

Normally, it's me being brave and Jag worrying about crocs and sharks and monsters of the deep. But out here alone in the dark, monsters of the deep is all I can think about! Every slosh of every wave is something leaping from the sea trying to sink *Licorice Stix* and eat me. But I keep on, away from the inland sea islands, past the sharp dark corners of the remaining towers of the old surf coast, and head north past Whaleback Ranges. I'm out to sea a bit, so I don't have to worry about not knowing exactly where the shoreline is, and to get a better view of where they might have stopped for the night.

I check the sky again and again, worried for those sudden hot storms that blow up out of nowhere. But the stars have taken over the whole sky. I say hello to the Milky Way, my home galaxy, that fuzzy stripe of light that stretches from one horizon to the other. She ain't so bright tonight coz the moon is almost full. I say hello to my kite-shaped friend the Southern Cross and her two pointer stars. She'll prolly dip below the horizon later, but I can find my way north now, with her pointing to the empty night sky that is south.

I pass the lights of the village of Blackberry and head up the coast some more. Blackberry has a red flashing light. The people of Blackberry din't pull their wires. 'Ain't no misbehaving kids in Blackberry,' I tell the wind.

One of the hulls thumps and rocks, like something soft is nudging it with a thud and a splash, and I sit low on the deck, hanging on to the wheel so hard my whole body is one white knuckle. It ain't whale season. This is it, the monsters people talk about, giant squids with tentacles longer than three boats, giant octopuses with reaching sucker-arms, stingrays with wing tips that can fold up either side of your boat, wrapping you up! And stranger things. Unknown things.

Licorice heaves. Drops. Carries on. A giant splash away to port, like something flipping its tail, leaving jus' a pounding in my chest. Maybe it was a really late whale heading south. Maybe it was a monster but not a hungry one. I dunno. I ain't good at imagining what could go wrong, on account of always leaving that side of things to Jag.

I pass the headland of Corky's Nob, where a solar light swings night and day to warn us of sharp rocks. There's rumours that on stormy nights Corky moves his light and boats hit rocks and Corky finds it easier than fishing or salvaging to pick up the pieces of the boats that smash on those rocks. You can always buy oarlocks and winches and other metal fittings and melted-down metal sinkers from Corky.

I dunno if Corky's moved the light tonight, so I take a wide trip around that headland. Ma's going to kill me anyway, but if I break *Licorice*, she'll make sure she kills me twice.

I pass the village of Five Sleeps. 'Five sleeps till what?' I ask the wind. 'And in what direction?'

The wind don't know any more than me.

A while later, I see what I'm looking for, a tiny light between Five Sleeps and Dog's Elbow. A pinprick of light on the shore where there's no village. I sail towards the light, then turn side on and adjust the sails so they don't flap or nothing to sail on by. It's harder than I thought to get a whole catamaran to be quiet. The ropes and wires creak, the mast groans, the winches slip, then there's waves slapping two hulls.

I grab *Licorice's* spyglasses, and study the light.

There's jus' the fronts of people, sitting by a fire, but their foreheads is glinting that gold sun, then a smaller person leans over and drops more driftwood on the fire, sending the fire sparking and sparkling with burning sand. A smaller person with a belt glinting with many useful tools. My best friend in all the world. My perfect numbat friend who would do this for me. Jaguar.

DOG'S ELBOW

Step One. Locate Jag. Done. All I have to do now is figure out how to get him back.

I drop the anchor out of Dog's Elbow, so I look like I've got business there, and when I'm sure it's firm, I open the top of the port-side hull and climb down onto the mattress that the littlies nap on if they ever come out fishing. It's nice down here, in the belly of the hull, walls all round, rocking in the dark.

When the sun wakes me through the open hatch, I scramble up with my spyglasses to see if the Valley of the Sun boat has left yet. It's gone from the beach, so I swing around the sea and look north, but it's nowhere.

Did it leave in the dark? Is it already gone over the horizon?

I put down the spyglasses and here it is. Tied to the jetty in Dog's Elbow. And up on the top of a nearby hill, people is already chopping trees into poles. *Thwop! Thwop! Thwop!* ringing out across the bay.

Up on the hill the two Valley men is working with Jag and about ten other people. They're getting it done a lot faster than they did at our village with all that help, that's for sure.

Down near the jetty, Gerra is sitting in the shade of a waterfront building and that bossy old woman ain't nowhere. Is Gerra looking right at me? Nah. She's still as a post.

What did Jag think when he sailed right past the *Licorice Stix*? Did he think Ma or Dizzy was up early following him, or his da maybe come to rescue him? Is he looking for them now in Dog's Elbow? We generally don't come to Dog's Elbow on account of their poor behaviour, them sometimes harbouring pirates and thieves, so Licorice Stix is never moored here. Us inland sea people, we don't see much of these main sea people. Already a man is rowing out to see what's up with me. Maybe hoping to trade or steal something, most prolly.

I turn on the little solar motor and move forward over the anchor to loosen it off, and pull it up. Then I run back to the deck, hoist the sail, and swing *Licorice* around. The man stands, wobbly in the dinghy, hand blocking the sun as he tries to figure out who's in this catamaran.

Most prolly Jag is the only one who knows *Licorice Stix* and where she's from. Most prolly he won't say a word. I don't think my cover is blown.

A CROC BY HIS TAIL

I sail away around the next headland as if I'm going further out to sea, and then turn back inland and look for somewhere to anchor.

There's a patch of sandy beach and a cliff face that looks like it's got a few goat trails up it, so I sail into the little bay and hunt around for a rock to anchor on, making my rescue plans. I don't want to leave the boat alone. Anyone could come and take it. But I have to see if I can get Jag back.

The only undersea rock I find is a bit far out from shore, and I don't want to swim all that way, or be so far from *Licorice* that I can't race back to move her if a boat comes around the headland. At least there's no one on this beach – it's protected by tall cliffs, which are a lot taller now I'm closer.

I dunno. Even if I do get Jag snuck away from the building work on the top of the hill, how can we get down the cliff and back into *Licorice* if she ain't been stolen, and away before the Valley of the Sun people get their boat around the headland? This is doomed. Maybe I should wait until dark?

Up on the beach the dark sand is moving . . . no, it's crocs. Dark sand-coloured dried-out crocs, sunning themselves. Seeing me in so close to their beach, they're coming to investigate. I'm definitely not getting off here. I don't even wanna hang about in the boat and have them swimming around me. These crocs ain't as huge as the ones near home. These is prolly young males, all driven out of good hunting spots by big ones, left to swim up and down the coast looking for a new home, resting where they can.

I sail up on the anchor I've only jus' hooked and try to work it free. The first of the crocs reaches me. It's only a bit taller than me if I lay down beside it, which I'd never do, not so scary. More arrive, larger ones, and circle *Licorice*. Now I get nervous. I go up to the bow to pull up the loose anchor, and find myself staring down into so many eyes, pale greenish speckledy eyes staring, leathery snouts bobbing in the water, trying to work out if I'm a meal. Their bodies hang down, straight down. They know they're easier to spot when they're swimming horizontal, so they hang in the water, tails down, pretending they're invisible.

'I see you!' I mutter, as I haul up the anchor. Then they do something I've never seen crocs do before. They sink out of sight. Jus' drop, like they're going down for a bit of a chat or something.

I lock the anchor and start back up the hull to the deck. There's a splash, and then a thump, and then a croc slides back into the sea behind me. It jumped right up onto the hull! I've never seen a croc this size try to jump into a boat. Normally that's a trick only the bigger ones try on tiny boats.

The next wave laps at the hull.

There's another splash, a thump, a splash, a thump! I run back to the deck. They've all learned to jump onto boats! The hulls is tall and they slide off, but there's three already on the netting between the hulls.

Their claws grab at the knotted ropes of the net and they's crawling up towards me.

I leap into the deck area, run up the sail and spin the boom about. I ain't sitting round to pick up more crocs. One teeters on the edge of the net and slides back into the water, but that leaves two with claws reaching, grabbing for the rope netting. One's feet fall through, first one front foot, then the other, and it's left with its front feet helplessly waving above the sea on the underside of the net. The other croc clambers over it, using it like a bridge, and keeps coming after me.

I winch the sail so it's taking me out to sea, and pick up my fish clubber. I can't believe that Jag was right about crocs jumping into boats!

This croc stumbles and slaps its tail, thumping the other croc in the head. It's still pushing itself towards me, muscly legs reaching, claws scraping, and mouth open showing rows of the large triangle teeth it wants to sink into me, but I dunno how it could get up and into the deck to get at me. Crocs ain't good at climbing on upright smooth surfaces like the bit of wall between the deck and the net.

I dunno whether to go and give it a thwack on the nose now, or wait and see if it can even get closer to me. I'll thwack it while there's a good hunk of wall between us. It's scraping its claws on the black fibreglass, head flopping side to side on the wall, not going anywhere, still thinking it can get to me this way. Crocs is cunning but also pretty stupid sometimes.

I lean over, swing hard and bop him on his nostrils with the fish clubber, and he turns tail and runs back over the stuck croc, right back out of the net, and sploshes into the sea with a massive tail flip.

I drop the sail. I'm far enough out now that the other crocs won't follow, but how do I get rid of this one?

I need to pee. Normally I jus' squat and pee through the net, but who can pee with a croc thrashing around down there?

I check for crocs and sharks, then hang out from the ladder attached to the stern of the boat we use for climbing out of the sea, pee, then go back and check the croc. He's got all four feet through the net now, and he's thrashing his tail and snapping his jaws like someone did it to him.

'You stuck yourself, you numbat!' I tell him.

I get out some dried fish and water and have a little breakfast while I wait to see if he can get himself free. Foot wiggling and head and tail thrashing gets him nowhere, and I can't see that he knows how to do anything else.

I scoop a bucket of water out of the sea and fling it at him. Crocs go in and out of the water to keep their temperature even and this one seems a bit hot. He opens his jaws wide and shows me all his teeth. 'You're going to have to get yourself out of this, Uncle Croc,' I tell him. 'Ain't much I can do. I ain't hauling no snapping croc out by his tail!'

FURTHER THAN
I'VE EVER GONE

I drop a fishing line while I wait for the croc to figure it out, and even though it takes a long time to hook my first fish, the croc's keeping on thrashing.

I've got the fish chunked and soaking in one of the jars of lime juice and coconut I brought with me, and still the croc's struggling. I throw a few more buckets of sea water over him, with him opening his jaws to warn me not to get too close. Then I throw him the fish skeleton, right into his open toothy jaws. He snaps them shut and rolls the kill roll, and that gets two of his feet out, and then he's a bucking, thrashing ball of fury with two feet and a tail, bashing around, angry that the other two feet is still tied up.

'Don't you break this net!' I yell at him. 'Ma will kill us both!'

A boat heading out to sea comes past the headland. I should be getting my sails up, croc or no croc, ready to speed away in case it comes to see what I'm about. But it don't turn my way. It keeps heading out to sea. Something glints off the prow. I grab the spyglasses, aim them across the sloshing blue sea, and finally slide across a pale hull. I move them back again and adjust the focus.

There's a golden sun on the prow, and five little heads. It's the Valley of the Sun boat! But where's it going? Even I know there ain't no land that way, not for a boat that size.

I throw the sail line on the winch and wind out the sail. Must be they's jus' going fishing, and they'll turn back once they get some fish for dinner.

I can't be on them like a tick, I gotta be on them like a croc, jus' my nose and eyeballs sticking out of the water to see where they's going. I gotta hang back. I swing the sail so it's jus' catching the wind. I'll plod along south of them until they head back in.

I dunno where Valley of the Sun is, I'm jus' thinking it's north, but what kind of people live in a valley since the risen sea anyway? Must be some massive sea wall that keeps a valley dry.

I spend the rest of the afternoon checking the Valley of the Sun boat with my spyglasses, chucking water on the croc who only moves when he gets a bit of water on him, and eating the chunks of fish as I sail along slowly heading out to sea.

The boat is too far away for me to know if they're casting lines. Too far even for me to see their heads through the spyglasses. But they keep trawling further and further out. Further than any boat of ours would usually dare go, so I'm happy to hang back.

Then I check and there is no boat. Jus' a dot of a sail on the horizon.

I turn to the croc. 'Uncle Croc, it may be that they ain't coming back. That they know of an island out there somewhere, and we're gonna have to move! There's pretty much no chance of you ever finding your way back to Dog's Elbow, so you best hang on.'

I swing the sail into the wind, and check the tell-tale woolies is blowing like they should, and hoist a jib sail too. I gotta get moving before I lose that speck of them!

I sail hard into the giant rolling waves of the open sea. *Licorice* creaks and groans and thumps the waves, and each one that hits the net smacks the poor croc in the belly. I chuck him some chunks of fish to make him less miserable. I can't eat it all. It only lasts a couple of days in the lime juice in this heat.

When I left home to chase down my friend Jag, I din't think I'd be attacked by crocs, and sailing further out to sea than I've ever gone.

LINES TO TAKE
ME HOME

As the earth turns away from the sun, I see a tiny light go up on the boat's mast which makes it easier for me to follow. I pull in the jib coz I've caught up close enough now to keep them in sight.

I'm kinda glad I gotta keep an eye on that croc, coz worrying about him getting loose and somehow getting up in here to make me into a meal will keep me awake. It's okay for them on the other boat, they can take it in turns to sail.

Me, alone cept for a no-good croc – it ain't fair. I won't be getting no sleep till we get where we're going.

But they keep sailing on and on into the night, and my eyes is dry from staring at that little light like a star on the water.

I wake with a jump, coz I din't mean to be asleep! *Licorice* is thumping, and it must be the croc trying to get over onto the deck to eat me. So I smash my arms around in the dark and leap to my feet all dreamy-brained and sleep-dizzy, trying to find my feet on the rolling dark sea. But there's no croc up here with me. I flick on my solar torch and check the net. The croc is lying quiet and still in the net, his eyes glowing in my torchlight, but something's still thumping the hulls. *Licorice* nudges over, and a huge splash sounds in the darkness.

I shine the torch in that direction. I think I see a massive tail, but it's gone in another splash.

There's a flash of paleness between the hulls, and the croc lifts up in the air. I swing the torch that way, and see the croc sitting on top of a big white nose, and rows and rows of white triangles. It's a shark!

A big shark. The biggest I've ever seen. The croc thrashes his head and tail, frees himself from the net and flops up close against the hull. Then he lies still, like a log. I turn off the torch and duck down too. Be a log. Don't be a tasty shark dinner. *Licorice* is still sailing, but

I can't see that light I was following no more. I could be sailing away in the wrong direction. I can't get the sail down and be a log at the same time. I gotta sit tight and wait till the shark decides there's no meal to be had here. It nudges and bumps poor *Licorice* for ages, while I hope it don't decide to take a bite of hull.

Finally, it lets off with its nudging and splashing.

I leap up and drop the sail on top of the boom, and get out my spyglasses. Nowhere on the horizon is that little bobbing light. I've lost Jag. I'll never find him now. I'll never save him. A grumpy old croc is the only kind of friend someone like me deserves.

I shine the light on the croc. He's still pretending to be a log in the corner hard up against the hull. He don't look like he's thinking about trying to get on deck to eat me. So I sit down and cry.

Down on the horizon, twinkling in the dark, sits the Southern Cross. I know I can turn *Licorice* home if I want – I jus' need to draw a line from the top of the Southern Cross down through the bottom and out, and then another line from the middle of the two bright stars that point to the Southern Cross, and where those two lines cross is the empty night sky of the south. I draw lines in the dark with my fingers. Lines to take me home.

I can turn *Licorice* south now and turn inland once the sun lights the horizon. But I don't want to give up on Jag.

So I tie down the sail and don't go nowhere.

PIRATES

I jump awake at a weird bang and a rattle. This time, I'd decided to nap, safe in the hull on my mattress. I might've run into something! I scramble out jus' as a woman screams.

It's morning, and standing on my netting is a woman with a big hat pulled down hard over her long scraggly grey hair, surprised eyes bulging out of her tanned and wrinkled face, waving a big knife.

There's a white yacht sailing nearby, all fibreglass patches of grey and cream and cracked wooden decking. 'Get off my boat!' I yell.

She looks at me like she din't expect to see a person.

'Call it off!' she screams, and takes a sideways dancing step away from Uncle Croc.

'No!' I say. 'You get off my boat right now or I tell him to attack!'

'Saleesi!' the woman calls, and a girl pops her shaved bald head up from behind the wheel of the yacht she's steering alongside *Licorice*.

'Hold on!' the girl calls. 'I'll get to whomping that rascal soon as I tie off.'

'Now!' the woman screeches at the girl, then turns back to me. 'We're salvaging this abandoned boat, so you and your pet gator need to get off!'

'Ain't no way I'm losing Ma's boat and getting into the sea with sharks,' I tell her. 'You leave right now or I tell my croc to bite your leg off.' I can't believe she thinks I have a pet croc.

'Well, if you don't want to get off my salvage, you can work for me,' the woman says, and puts her hands on her hips.

And Uncle Croc's waving his jaws around, but he ain't attacking like I spect. I lean over to check he's not got his legs caught again, but it seems like he's figured out the netting now.

'Get 'er!' I yell at him.

Uncle Croc thrashes his tail like he's got a mind to eat this old lady but she's too fast for him. She makes two giant leaps across the net and then she's over the wall and standing in front of me.

'You can't salvage this boat, coz it's mine!' I tell her.

'Well, ain't you precious,' the old woman says, and smirks. 'Likely you stole it from some fisher village up the coast and I'll be able to trade it back and live a fine life for a while, thank you very much.'

'It ain't stole. It's my ma's boat and she'll come looking for it real soon.'

She grabs my hand and turns it palm up, runs her grimy rough hands over it. 'You ain't got no ma. Look at them rough hands, them bruises, look at that graze on your head. Ain't no one looked after you in a while. But don't worry, little wormy-mouth, you're in Aunty Bradshaw's family now.'

I pull my hand back. 'That's not true! This is my boat, and I'm taking it home to my ma!'

'Saleesi!' the woman yells, and the girl from the yacht swings in on a rope and lands on the deck in front of me, hands on hips. This girl is taller than me but skinny and built of muscles. 'Yes, Pirate Bradshaw?'

'Pirate?' I ask. She's a *pirate*? Me and my boat are now in pirate hands?

'She's jus' funning. I ain't no pirate,' the old woman says, and pulls me close, breathes a hot fishy-stink over me. 'Now you wanna join my crew and work your passage back to land or you want to get off here?'

'I ain't getting off!' I say.

'Good choice. Welcome to the crew. Saleesi will take you aboard while I tie off my salvage.'

'This ain't your salvage!' I say to Pirate Bradshaw's back, coz she's already reaching for *Licorice's* tie-off ropes.

Saleesi grabs my arm with fingers like wire and wraps a rope around my middle. 'Ain't no point in arguing with her. You'll give her a headache and then she'll be mean as a cut snake to both of us,' she says, hitching the rope up to my armpits.

'But she's stealing my boat,' I say.

'Yep, she stole my boat and prolly et my da, so you're not so bad off, eh?' She blinks her dark eyes jus' once, like she got some emotions buried about that. I don't think that old pirate ate her da, but maybe she's on my side.

'Then help me stop her,' I whisper.

'Ain't no stopping her. I'm not even sure she's flesh and bone like the rest of us. Come on.' Saleesi hoists me up onto *Licorice's* seat. 'Monkey on up the side of our yacht,' she says.

I don't wanna, but Saleesi's rope is hooked around a pulley on the mast of their scrappy yacht and whether I want to climb or not she's hauling me up, and I gotta jus' use my hands and feet to keep from being dragged up the hull of their boat.

I land on their splintery deck and work at the rope under my armpits, coz I gotta get back to *Licorice*. I gotta go on and look for Jag. I got no choice.

Then I'm hauled up again for jus' a moment and Saleesi swings in beside me.

'I gotta get away. I gotta rescue my friend,' I whisper.

'S'you who needs rescuing right now. Quit flapping yer gums and get these sails hauled up before she gets back on board.'

'I ain't hauling your sails. I'm getting out of here!' I climb back over the yacht's railing.

'More front than a Jakarta sea wall, you,' Saleesi says, and gets busy hauling the rope.

I leap for *Licorice's* hull but my shirt is yanked back, collar tight across my throat. Out of nowhere a hand swings me by the shirt in a choking, armpit-cutting circle back onto the yacht. I'm dumped on my butt before I can even take another breath.

Pirate Bradshaw stands over me. 'I thought we had an agreement? You crew for me, I take you back to land. You skiving off already? I'm gonna dock your pay. You owe me two hours work.'

'I din't cost you two hours!'

'Punishment. Don't let me catch you skiving again or I'll take what's left of your hair to sell at the market.'

I look at Saleesi. She shrugs and points at a slack rope. I run and pull it tight, cleat it off and tie the ends out of the way.

'Much better,' Pirate Bradshaw says. 'Now I want this whole deck sanded and oiled before we hit shore. The slower you sand, the slower I sail. If you don't do it at all, we'll be at sea until you're older than me, lovey!'

The deck wood is white with age and cracked and splintered like it never met a coat of oil in its life, a bit like the old pirate's face. 'It's going to take days!' I complain.

Saleesi shakes her head at me.

Pirate Bradshaw squints. 'Is you moaning at me, you little wormy-mouthed boat-thief? Me what takes you in, gives you a home and a bed and a real job?'

'She ain't moaning, Pirate Bradshaw,' Saleesi says quickly.

'Shuddup. She can answer. She's done nothing but stand around flapping her gums.'

'Where's the sandpaper?' I say. 'I'm itching to get started.'

Pirate Bradshaw shoves Saleesi in the stomach, making her go, 'Oof!' and bend double. 'She's quicker than you,' Bradshaw says to the back of Saleesi's bald head. 'You wanna watch she don't steal your job.'

The old pirate reaches under the seat and throws a pile of sandpaper, most of it used already, at my feet. I drop to my knees and grab a hunk and rub at the splintery deck boards.

Saleesi kneels beside me and picks up some sandpaper too.

'I'm sorry,' I whisper.

'You ain't done it. She wants me to hate you, so I'm gonna yell at you now,' Saleesi whispers. Then she yells, 'Shuddup!'

Pirate Bradshaw takes the wheel and chomps on salted sardines as she steers the yacht in a direction I guess as north, looking at where the sun is.

I keep glancing back at where *Licorice Stix* is jerking along through the waves behind. I could run and dive and be on her in seconds, but how do I stop Pirate Bradshaw from jus' taking her back off me?

'Stop looking at yer boat and planning things,' Saleesi whispers.

'I'm not,' I say. But I is. Maybe the old pirate will go to sleep and I can sneak away. Sail off in the dark. *Licorice Stix* is hard to see in the dark.

AND TRICKSTERS

We sand for hours. My fingers are sore and full of splinters, my arm muscles are almost too tired to go on. We don't stop for water or food, and finally Pirate Bradshaw throws some rags at us. 'Wipe all that dust off!' she says. 'Then you can start on the oil.'

'Can I go feed my croc?' I ask, coz I know there's food and water on *Licorice*.

'Crocs don't need to eat every day.'

'But I gotta throw water on him to keep him cool,' I say.

'It can dip itself in the sea. Or are its legs broken?'

'Yep, it can't move at all. Why else it jus' be sitting on a boat.'

'You fixing to eat it? That why you wanna plump it up?'

'No!' I say coz the idea of eating Uncle Croc is jus' weird now we've sailed together for a couple of days.

'Then you don't need to feed it. Do the oil and keep your wormy-mouth shut,' Pirate Bradshaw says and shoves me away.

Saleesi and I mop away the dust and then get to rubbing the oil into the boards. They turn dark and shiny like they's enjoying being cared for after so long. We're still working as the earth turns away from the sun. Pirate Bradshaw's gone below and she's cooking up a feast by the smell of things. My stomach growls.

'She ain't cooking for you,' Saleesi says.

'But I worked all day for her,' I say.

'Still, don't you take her food, or you'll be for it,' Saleesi says.

'Oh, my faithful crew!' Pirate Bradshaw calls in a strange sweet voice and my feet are carrying my stomach to the door to below before I can stop them.

On the table sitting in a frypan is a large fish floating in rich red sauce, and it smells amazing. 'Come on down now. Work done for the day. Eat up!' She hefts a hunk of fish onto a metal plate and lays a fork beside it. 'Come on, it's getting cold.' She sets a jug of water on the table too.

I'm straight down there. It's a matter of life or death. I spent a long day sweating in the hot sun and I gotta drink. I gulp down two cups of water and shovel that fish in so fast, it's almost gone by the time Pirate Bradshaw sits down.

'Where's Saleesi?' I ask.

'Ungrateful thing don't like my cooking. Your bunkroom is through the back if you wanna lie down,' she says, and waves at a little door beside the steps back up to the deck.

I finish all my food and I'm thinking I'll sleep now so I can get up early, unhitch *Licorice Stix* and sail away before Pirate Bradshaw wakes up.

'Thank you,' I say coz I don't want her to call me ungrateful thing, and head to the little wooden door. There's jus' room enough to stand up in there, and the rest is a long thin bed with a blanket on it. I crawl onto the bed and lay down. Then there's a click. She's locked the door! I crawl back and hammer on the door. 'Let me out!' She don't answer. Above the bed there's a hatch but no amount of pushing on it will move it. It's also locked from the outside. I'm stuck here, on a pirate boat. How can I ever get home? How will I rescue Jag?

TERRIFIED TO
MY BONES

I wanna cry so I try telling myself the good things. It's good she ain't taken *Licorice* and sailed off. It's good I got a full belly and a nice place to sleep. It's good she'll need me on deck tomorrow to keep sanding and I'll get another chance to escape. I feel a bit calmer then and yawn coz I'm real tired. I'll need lots of sleep to get energy to escape.

The lock clicks at first light and Pirate Bradshaw stands at the door. 'Get up!' she says. 'There's work to be done! Let's see, cabin hire, and a meal, two cups of water. I reckon you owe me about four days' work.'

'What?' I ask, following her up top. 'You gave me food, you locked me in. I ain't paying for that.'

'You wanna get off here then?' she asks.

There's a wide wide expanse of risen sea lying all the way to where the edge of the planet's turning to meet the red sun. And there's way worse out there than Pirate Bradshaw. That's for sure. 'No,' I say.

'Good. Then work!' Pirate Bradshaw says, and I drop to the deck beside Saleesi and we rub wooden boards with sandpaper.

'Where were you last night?' I whisper.

'Don't take nothing from her. She keeps a tally. She'll own you forever,' Saleesi says.

'But what do you eat? Where do you sleep?' I ask.

'On the deck. She still charges me for that but jus' half a day's work, and I fish for my own dinner. I take a cup of water if I run out of storm water that I save when it's running off the deck. She charges half a day for water.'

'But that's not fair – she's charging more to work here than we can earn!'

Saleesi shrugs. 'First I took everything, coz I was gonna kill her, and I wouldn't have no debt. But then I found out she don't die so easy.'

'Well, she better not stand between me and *Licorice Stix* or she'll be for it,' I say.

'Stop your muttering, you wormy-mouthed kid, and get this deck looking shipshape!' Pirate Bradshaw yells.

Saleesi and I sand the deck all day with the sun beating my bare scalp, my back through my shirt, burning. Ma would be chasing me down with a hat by now. Tears squirm in my eyes. I gotta not think about my ma. I gotta think about how to get out of here.

It's late in the afternoon and I'm feeling dizzy when a man shouts, 'Hello!'

I stagger up and there's a fishing boat pulling alongside. Then Pirate Bradshaw grabs me, hauls me across the deck and drops me through a hatch to below. I land on the mattress as the hatch slams above me. 'Let me out. Help me!' I yell.

Pirate Bradshaw stomps her feet on the hatch door. No one will hear me over that.

'Ahoy, sirs! Might you be looking for a neat new fishing catamaran?' she yells.

'No!' I scream. 'It's mine! Not hers!'

Stomp! Stomp! Stomp! The old pirate's feet beat like a drum on the hatch lid. I push open the cabin door, and try the door to up top, but it's latched from the outside. I scramble over junk and work at the porthole latches. They's bubbled and white and stiff with salt and age. Old and ruined, like everything on this old yacht. I try the other hatches, also locked.

'Saleesi!' I yell. 'Tell them we're prisoners!'

Stomp! Stomp! Stomp!

I splash my face and drink as much water as I can, while listening to what's going on up top. Pirate Bradshaw seems to be negotiating with the fishermen. For fish and lines and nets and gear, I hear. Something about a gold ring one of the fishermen has on. I can't tell what's going on. I fill my pockets with biscuits, and a carrot. Now they's shouting!

'Never! You wrinkly old salt!' one of the men shouts clear as anything.

Then there's silence.

'Saleesi!' Pirate Bradshaw says.

'Saleesi!' I yell. 'Tell them I'm a fisher from Cottage Hill. Tell them to tell my ma where I am!'

There's no stomping this time. So I carry on. 'I'm Neoma from Cottage Hill! *Licorice Stix* is my boat. She's not for sale!'

The yacht creaks and groans and ropes run through winches, then it tips over and slaps at the sea. It's moving! Oh no! They've sold *Licorice Stix*. We're leaving her behind! I hammer at the door to up top.

Saleesi opens it. 'I din't know you were a fisher,' she says, like she heard me this whole time and still she let them take my boat.

I push past her and run to the stern. *Licorice* is still there! She's tied up behind the little fishing boat tied to the back of the yacht! Not a fisherman to be seen.

'What?' I say.

'Lots to salvage out here,' Pirate Bradshaw says. She's wearing a new ring.

I don't see no fishermen swimming in the sea behind us.

Pirate Bradshaw reaches over her shoulder and plucks a thin fish filleting knife from her back. 'Ooch!' she says. She wipes the blood off on her trousers and runs a finger along the blade. Nods, and slides it into a strap on her leg.

'What happened?' I ask.

'We couldn't come to an agreement,' Pirate Bradshaw says. 'Now get back to work.'

Me and Saleesi carry on with our sanding like everything's normal. 'Where's the fishermen?' I whisper.

'Where'dya think?' she says.

I don't wanna think. I give her a biscuit from my pocket. She swallows it in two bites.

When the planet turns from the sun, and the cool sets in, Pirate Bradshaw gets to cooking again. Delicious smells floating up from below and out across the water.

'Crew!' she calls sweetly. 'Come down for dinner.'

I break the carrot I stole earlier in half and give half to Saleesi. We chomp them real fast.

Pirate Bradshaw pops her head up on deck after a while. 'Anyone hungry?' she asks.

'I'm too tired,' I say. 'I'm jus' gonna sleep on the deck.'

I lie down beside Saleesi and pretend to sleep.

'Nice night for it,' Pirate Bradshaw says and lies herself on a seat in the stern.

This means I gotta sneak past her to get to *Licorice*. I lie looking up at the Milky Way, locating my old friend the Southern Cross and her pointer stars, find that patch of blank dark sky that marks south where I gotta be heading. Two days sailing north don't do me much good for finding Jag. My head is hot, my back is hot, my hands are worn and burning, and I'm terrified to my bones that the old hag Bradshaw will kill me if she catches me escaping.

Saleesi pulls a bit of jib sail over us to keep the breeze from waking us, and soon she's asleep.

BUBBLES RISING
FROM THE DEEP

I crawl out from under the sail and tiptoe down to the stern of the boat. There's only starlight, so things is jus' outlines, but Pirate Bradshaw is honking up a snore like a flock of geese chasing a dog. No way she'll hear me. I climb down the ladder behind the cockpit and start working at the knot tying the fishing boat on. There's a swish by my ear and the knot judders in my hands. There's a knife sticking out of it!

'What're you doing?' Pirate Bradshaw asks.

'Jus' having a pee!' I squeak. Can she see in the dark? So then I pee, climb back up, and walk past Pirate Bradshaw sitting there, picking her teeth with another knife, making a scraping sound, prolly meant to warn me.

I lie down again next to Saleesi.

'She got the senses of a wild cat,' Saleesi whispers. And I gotta admit, much as I feel sorry for Saleesi stuck here with this old pirate, I'm getting a bit mad about all her warnings and not doing anything to help me.

I wait until the Southern Cross is long gone from the night sky and then try again. Pirate Bradshaw's snoring like a goose but then she's not, and she's on the ladder above me. 'You got bladder problems, kid?' she says.

'Maybe,' I say coz I think there's a chance she hasn't guessed what I'm doing here.

'You wake me again tonight and you won't have no problems no more,' she says.

'Yes sir, Pirate Bradshaw,' I say, and hurry back under the sail.

I sleep this time, till I'm kicked awake by Pirate Bradshaw. 'I reckon you'll get the deck finished today,' she says, all cheerful. 'Up and at 'em!'

It's midday and a half day's sailing in the wrong direction when we finally get the deck wood all oiled and shiny. It looks like a whole new boat from where I'm standing holding the last of the oil.

Pirate Bradshaw does an inspection, her wrinkled and cracked toes rubbing the wood looking for splinters. Finally she nods. 'Good job. Now I got another job for you,' she says, and heads back to where I'm standing next to the steering wheel. I know where she's gonna step. She's gonna step on the edge of the cockpit and down onto the seat. I got the oil in my hand and she's busy telling Saleesi to fetch some tools, so I pour a little oil on the cockpit edge, and I pour a little oil on the seat and then I go stand next to the ladder at the stern.

Pirate Bradshaw looks up at me as she's coming back to the cockpit. 'Gotta pee again?' she says, then she hits the edge of the cockpit, her foot slides, she steps heavily down onto the seat and that foot slides too. She tips, she falls, I throw the oil, scramble down the ladder and untie the fishing boat. There's a clatter of metal and a thump of body as I pull the fishing boat closer and leap aboard.

'Come on, Saleesi!' I yell. But I won't wait for her. I got one chance to get away and Saleesi ain't helped me none. She can swim for it if she wants to leave with me.

I run flat out for the stern of the fishing boat. There's a bunghole there for when it's pulled out of the sea and washed clean of fish blood and such, so I stop a moment to unscrew it, and seawater gushes in. I pull *Licorice* in and untie her, and leap aboard, so all three boats is now separated by sea and floating apart.

Mr Croc is asleep in the net, poor thing, looking hot and miserable. I run up the hull before he even gets a few steps towards me. Then I'm back on my deck, hauling the sail and throwing the solar motor on, to get some space from that old pirate.

I've done it. I'm free. The fishing boat between us is low in the water, and there's no sign of Pirate Bradshaw.

Saleesi stands on the yacht looking at me.

'Come on!' I yell.

Then there's a splash, and Pirate Bradshaw is once again standing, hands on hips, dripping wet, on the net in front of me. Only a hull wall, a bit of net and a tired crocodile between us.

'You're an ungrateful thief,' she says.

'*Licorice Stix* is mine!' I tell her.

The croc ain't lunging at her like I thought he might, but he has his mouth open like he's warning her not to make a move. Three days of no food has prolly made him weak.

I take my jar of fish in lime and coconut and throw a chunk on his nose. He snaps at it. Misses. Lets it fall right through the net to the sea. Then I take a whole handful of fish chunks, and jus' as Pirate Bradshaw takes a few steps across the net towards me and asks, 'Is that how you train him?', I fling them at her. They smash into her chest and belly and drip down her front.

She gasps, and gasps again when the croc whips his tail and lunges at her. She turns to run, scrambling along the net back towards the sea. The croc lunges after her, snaps his jaws around her leg and they tumble into the sea together.

I can't say I'm unhappy to see them go, but the sight of seeing the croc launch like that, all his back and tail muscles flexing so fast and his jaws snapping, have given me the shivers. I never saw a croc get no one before, and I'd got to thinking this one was friendly.

Saleesi's leaning over the edge of the yacht, watching the water. She's smiling. Jus' quietly at first, then she laughs when the croc's tail goes splashing past, and the water turns red.

'Oh no!' I say, coz I don't want the old pirate killed, nor my croc. The croc and me have a bit of a friendship going.

'Oh yes!' Saleesi says, when neither woman nor croc come to the surface, and then something rises. It's Pirate Bradshaw swimming back up. She's killed my grumpy pal with her knife. But it's only her hat that breaks the surface and sits there. Ain't no head following it up for a gulp of air.

I run out on the net, lean over and lift the hat. Nothing underneath. Jus' bubbles rising from the deep. I got a bad feeling. It's one of those times when strange things happen to set the day crooked, like crabs in dolls' heads, and strangers sailing out of the mist.

'We gotta wait a while,' Saleesi says.

'What?' I ask.

'That old sea hag can hold her breath for ages. She got gills, I reckon. And she can prolly bite harder than that croc. It'll let go. Either of us sail off and leave her here still alive, she'll come after both of us and make us pay, specially if she has to swim for hours through shark-infested waters to do it.' Saleesi waves to where the fishing boat is now leaning over and disappearing into the sea after the pirate and the croc.

'I don't have to wait,' I say. I jump up and run back to the deck, wind the sail line around the winch, pull it tight.

'Aren't you gonna wait for your gator to come back?' Saleesi asks.

'No way,' I say, and swing the boom.

'Wait!' she says. 'Where you going?'

'Why should I tell you?' I ask.

'Coz maybe I wanna come with you?'

'You were helping her steal my boat.'

'Nah, that old pirate? I don't wanna help her no more than I wanna battle your croc.'

'Yeah? Well, I ain't waiting round to see if she's still alive.' I turn *Licorice* about.

'Hey!' Saleesi says. 'I could help you! Wasn't we getting along?'

'You din't help me escape once. I don't need your help now,' I say and sail off.

'Then why was you drifting out here all alone on the wide sea in the first place?' she calls.

'I'm off to rescue a friend,' I yell.

Saleesi sets to turning the yacht about. 'Jus' so happens rescuing is what I do best!'

I don't listen to her. There's lots of dodgy people on the risen sea, and I ain't gonna be tricked out of *Licorice*, no how, no way.

COMPLETELY EMPTY

I sail south towards who knows where, but anywhere away from pirates. I could do with my friend Jag backing me up here. I'm the doer. He's the one who's cautious, 'cept when he goes and takes my place in the Valley of the Sun boat. He's the one who'd tell me for sure if Saleesi is a trickster working for the pirate or not. Saleesi might know which way the Valley of the Sun is from sailing round pirating for so long, but she might lie to trick me.

She's following. She's slower to get moving, got a heavier boat, so I don't think she'll catch up anytime soon. It's a couple of hours before I lose her completely. She's got her own boat now. She'll be fine.

I head south by keeping the afternoon sun to starboard, but I'm way out to sea so I'm really lost about how far up the coast I've come in the last few days.

I'm quicker than that old pirate yacht so I don't have to worry about them no more. Especially since Pirate Bradshaw is long dead. I sail till the earth turns away from the sun and my old star-friends dot the sky and I can sail more accurately in a straight line south. I eat some of my dried fish, I drink, I have short sleeps but keep waking to check the stars. Then when the earth turns back to the sun, I wash myself in the sea to wake myself up.

I'm still going looking for Jag. This is why I'm out here, after all. I gotta head back in, find a village, ask there for how to find the Valley of the Sun.

After a while I find some fishing boats sitting with their lines out, so I wave to them and pull alongside.

'Sir!' I call out to an old man. 'Can you help me figure out which way is the Valley of the Sun?'

The old guy pulls his hat off, tilts his head, and wipes his wispy grey hair over his brown, but not as brown as his face, scalp. 'Last I saw it was that way,' he says and points back out.

'But I been out there,' I say.

'You'll know you're getting close when you see the mist,' he says. 'Did you see the mist?'

I shake my head.

'It's not an easy place to find,' he says. 'Specially if you're sailing alone.'

'I ain't sailing alone. My da and uncle is sleeping down in the hulls,' I say.

The man shrugs. 'Just the way you said you been out there, not we been out there, makes me think you should be careful going near the Valley of the Sun. I don't wanna see you lose that pretty little fishing boat.'

'No sir,' I say. '*We* won't lose it. *We* jus' got some business in Valley of the Sun. Thank you for your help. Go gentle.'

I spin about and head back out, casting some lines as I go to take advantage of the schools of fish I'm passing. I immediately pull in two large fish and kill them and drop them in my bucket for later. Don't usually go deep sea fishing, but this is easy.

It don't feel safe to be heading directly out from the coast alone. I'm a land critter, but the Valley of the Sun boat went this way somewhere, and it's no more suited to crossing oceans than *Licorice Stix*. I keep checking the horizon coz my detour into land and back out again means Saleesi could have caught up, but no sails anywhere. Saleesi must've given up following me and gone somewhere else. Good.

I'm squeezing limes to get fish soaking when a scream rattles my skull. First I think that old pirate's been swimming after my boat to teach me a lesson for setting my croc on her and this is her killing scream. But no sea hag leaps on board to kill me, and the scream peels back my ears again.

I stand up on the port hull, can't see nothing. I bounce across the net to the starboard hull and there, sitting in the water, clinging to a chunk of wood, is Saleesi. A fin is circling her in the water, and every now and then she stabs out with the chunk of wood. 'I'm gonna whomp you!' she tells the shark.

I grab a coil of rope, hang on to one end, haul back my arm and send it spinning and unfurling through the air. It lands in front of her. She swims and grabs it and wraps it around her body as I wrap my end around the winch. By the time it snaps tight from the speed the Licorice is travelling at, she's tied it off, leaving her hands free to swing that hunk of wood at the shark.

Saleesi submerges a bit as she's jerked along behind *Licorice*, then pops up with a big old mama shark following. I turn on the winch. Saleesi smacks the shark with her bit of wood and skips across the surface on her behind, her legs pulled up, away from the chasing shark. A massive mouth, all gums and rows of chomping teeth, rises out of the water jus' behind her. She screams as a whole shark rises up above her. The shark's eyes is closed, so she's jus' chomping, chomping at the air, wondering where her meal is at, fat body and tail jerking back and forth, pushing her high up out of the water. The old thing is the size of a whale!

My heart thumps and my legs wobble like they're telling me to run, like they forgot I'm on a boat and running off the boat would be bad right about now. The giant shark falls, falling sideways onto Saleesi. But *Licorice Stix* acts like she seen the shark too, and she keeps powering through the sea, and the winch keeps grinding away sure and steady and the shark falls short, crashing into the sea, sending a wave up and swamping over Saleesi's shaved head.

I run to the starboard hull she's prolly gonna hit, coz ain't no one there to shut the winch off. Saleesi pops out of the sea again, blinking and gasping like someone who almost got swallowed whole by a giant shark, still swishing that hunk of wood around with one arm. I hang off a stanchion and throw out my hand. 'Come on!' I yell, like there's anything she can do right now to get aboard quicker.

Deep down below there's a shadow about the length of the starboard hull with a tail. It turns and points up at us. 'Hurry!' I scream.

Saleesi reaches out her arm like she can get to me, but the shape down below, now half white, half dark, with its face opening up into flashes of pointy teeth, that monster shark is moving faster than anything I ever seen. My eyes swell with the sight of it, and when something grabs my outstretched hand, I pull back like it's the shark herself. But that shark, with a wash of water in front of it, pushes up and up through the surface of the sea and douses me in a massive wave, sending me surfing right over the deck, right over the deck wall, bouncing into the net, and then there's teeth high above the hull gnashing on wood, and wood splintering and flying, and I got nothing in my hand! Did fear make me let Saleesi go? Was she swallowed whole? And the shark veers away from *Licorice* and smashes back into the sea sending another wave swamping the boat, up through the net, lifting me for a moment so I'm washed back towards the deck, coz *Licorice* is still powering away like she knows we gotta get out of here.

I'm dropped back onto the net, hard up against the hull where my croc lay, and there's silence, jus' the winch still cranking and a noise like *flak, flak, flak*. I crawl up the wall between net and deck and there's the winch, rope still in a loop going round and round, completely empty. Oh no!

OLD MAMA SHARK

Then the net below me pushes up again and the dark body of the shark lifts the middle. She's still here, looking for another feed, her slimy skin sliding against my knees. I scramble over the wall onto the deck. And the deck is soft and wet and grumbles, 'Ooof!' and it's Saleesi.

She's been dragged all the way to the deck and pulled the rope off herself. But there's blood, a lot of blood, and water smearing it everywhere, making it run bright in the grooves between the boards on the dark deck of *Licorice*. I scramble off her. She's still got two legs and arms, so that's good.

'What happened?' I ask.

'I tol' you. I tol' you, you don't cross that old sea hag, Pirate Bradshaw. She swam after me and threw me off her boat for stealing it away while she was busy fighting your croc.' Saleesi is holding her hand with her other hand.

'Did the shark bite your hand?' I ask. Saleesi holds her left hand up and her middle finger is missing from the knuckle on. 'Pirate Bradshaw chopped it off and threw it and me to the sharks.'

'Lucky you had that bit of wood to fight it off.'

'That wasn't no bit of wood. That was the rudder. After she threw me off the side, I clung to the rudder so hard she chopped that off as well and left me floating on the sea.'

Licorice Stix thuds and rocks. That shark knows where her meal went.

I block up the bunghole with a lime skin to stop the blood leaking off the deck, prolly sending signals to every shark in the risen sea to come here for a meal, and grab a rag for Saleesi to wind around her finger end. 'Stop bleeding everywhere,' I tell her.

'S'your fault. Had you let me come with you, we coulda left the pirate's boat for her, and we coulda sped off without her. Why you grouchy wif me? I'm the one what almost got et by a giant shark!'

The shark gives the hull of *Licorice* another good nudge and circles her to see what falls off. We crouch low on the deck.

'You jus' tol' me stories about how I couldn't escape. You never helped me and I din't tell you to come chasing after me, did I?' I say. 'I got my own problems.'

Saleesi screws up her face as she winds the rag tight around her finger. 'Oh right, you gotta rescue someone.'

'Yeah. I do,' I say. 'So you jus' better not be bringing me no trouble.'

'I tol' you. Rescuing is my speciality. First thing you want to do is set your sail a bit to starboard, or you're gonna sail right on by Valley of the Sun.'

'How do you know where I'm going?'

'It's the only place out here.'

'You've been there?'

Saleesi nods. 'Yep, we was there five days ago trading.' She stands up, hanging tight to the edge of the deck wall in case the shark nudges again. I stand too. She points a bit south-east. 'Then it was about there. But by now, it'll be over there.' She points east.

'It moves?' I ask.

Saleesi laughs and laughs until her finger aches and then she groans and holds her sopping, bloody rag-wrapped hand to her chest. 'You're going to be a stunned mullet when you see it,' she says.

The shark gives us another nudge, then turns suddenly and heads off, tall fin cutting through the slopping waves.

THEY'RE BACK!

Saleesi won't tell me nothing more about Valley of the Sun coz she says it'll ruin the surprise, so I ignore her and go back to cutting up the fish and putting chunks in two jars of lime, coconut juice and chilli. She steals chunks jus' raw and chucks them in her mouth and picks off the skeleton with her teeth like raw fish is the tastiest meal ever.

'Don't you cook fish where you're from?' I ask.

'You ain't cooking, you is jus' soaking.'

'It's a kind of cooking. It makes the meat softer and more flavourful.'

'Ooh, more flavourful! You're some kind of fancy-pants, ain'tcha?' Saleesi says.

I get hot then. 'I ain't fancy. I'm a hardworking fisher, and I know what makes fish taste best.'

'And I know what fills my belly.' Saleesi mashes big chunks of raw fish in her face with her good hand and grins so fish meat squeezes out between her teeth.

I laugh coz she looks silly, even if she is the most annoying person ever. I slap her fish-chunk-thieving hand. 'Jus' wait till it's done!' and I scoop the rest of the fish chunks into two jars. 'It takes a while for the lime to work into the meat.' I'm glad I caught big fish now I got another mouth to feed.

I fetch the first-aid kit, and make sure Saleesi's finger is clean and wrapped up properly. Her chin is set hard and a tear rolls down her face, but she don't complain once. She's pretty staunch. She's also really skinny after jus' feeding herself on Pirate Bradshaw's boat, so no wonder she was shoving that raw fish in like she never had no breakfast.

Now she's not bleeding and the fish is done, I haul up a bucket of sea water to wash down the deck. If Ma saw the deck of *Licorice* in this state, she'd be mad. I take off my hat, wash down my face, head and hands to cool me off.

'What's wrong with your head?' Saleesi asks.

Her head is sitting there, almost bald. I don't think she should be making fun of people with injuries.

'I forgot my hat one day and the sun burnt my hair right off,' I say.

Saleesi frowns and runs her hand over her own head.

'You wanna get a hat,' I say. 'There'll be a spare down in the hull.'

Jus' as I pick up the chopping board to scrape the fish carcasses into the sea, Saleesi yells, 'Shark's back!'

Saleesi's got a white-knuckle grip on the deck wall, coz that shark's fin is cutting through the sea, water bulging ahead of it, running at us at a great speed, head on!

The shark being as big as one hull of *Licorice*, I don't want her to hit us full on. It might sink us.

I drop everything and hammer on the bell we keep for when we're sailing in fog, coz maybe old mama shark ain't seen us, but she don't turn away and I dunno what to do. If I turn away, she'll strike one of the hulls and make a hole for sure, so I jus' keep on hammering on the bell and watching her coming head on.

'Get down and hang on!' I yell to Saleesi. Her face is pale as anything as she drops to the floor and hooks her good arm through the steering wheel. I dive down and do the same thing.

There's a *whomp! Licorice* dives, and we, still clinging to the wheel near the stern, pop up high in the air as the nose of the boat dips into the sea. We slide forward. Saleesi screams. And the sight I see is one I can't hardly understand. There's a giant shark tail thrashing up in the air, but coming up over the deck wall is a snapping croc head, and our legs are slipping out from under us, sliding down to meet both these things we never wanna meet in our whole lives ever. Fish carcasses and blood and us, all sliding towards two things that wanna eat us and *Licorice* diving down nose first to meet them.

Then *Licorice* bucks and with a terrible heave the shark flicks her mighty tail and flings herself back into the sea. *Licorice* pops back up, bounces and rocks, boom swinging side to side, so we stay low and hang on until she rights herself.

There's this moment of calm. The breeze catches the sail and it swings back to where it should be with a waloompf, wind fills the sail and *Licorice* creaks as she pulls herself around to carry on the way she was going. The steady *slop, slop, slop* of sea waves beats on her hulls and I kick off a fish carcass and pull myself up.

I help Saleesi up, coz she's looking sick. The hull thumps and rocks, and a fin glides away from the boat again.

'That shark's pretty angry that this boat stole two good meals from her,' she says, and points into the net. 'Yer gator's back.'

'He's not mine,' I say. 'I got no control over what he does. He'd eat me soon as look at me.' It's gotta be the same croc, coz there's no reason for a sea croc to be this far from shore unless he chased a pirate off a boat, and besides, he's got her big knife buried tip-deep in his skull. 'Well, that's not very nice,' I say. I look around for sails, scared that if Uncle Croc can find us, Pirate Bradshaw can too.

'She'll be mad about losing that cutlass. That's her favourite,' Saleesi says.

'The croc is jus' doing what crocs do, ain't no call to leave him swimming around maimed.'

The croc opens his mouth to warn me not to try anything, like I even could.

The frame that holds the net is dipping at the front where the shark landed on it, and my heart sinks. Ma is gonna be so mad at me about that. Metal's not as strong once it's been bent and unbent. The rust will get in.

The shark nudges the boat again, pushing it sideways.

'Go away or I'll whomp you!' Saleesi screams.

One of the jars of fish has broken and fish chunks is all over the deck along with the glass fragments threatening to stick our feet. My bucket, the water what was in it, the fish carcasses and their blood and guts, lime skins and coconut juice, and Saleesi's finger blood, all sloshing around in a terrible mess. So all I can do is rescue the jar that's whole, and we sit on a seat and eat fish chunks until the shark decides neither the croc nor Saleesi is gonna come back to her.

Then I sweep everything into a pile, pull the lime skin bung to let all the liquids run out, and fish out the carcasses and fish chunks. I feed them to Uncle Croc while Saleesi hooks a rope over that big ol' knife.

The croc is so exhausted from out-swimming giant sharks he jus' lies there with his mouth wide letting me chuck everything in, barely snapping shut now and then to swallow. But when Saleesi hooks the rope now tied to the knife over the boom and pulls tight, yanking it from in his skull, he goes into a struggling frenzy, snapping his head this way and that, making the knife pop out and go flying up. Saleesi snaffles it right out of the air with a quick grab and jams it in her belt like a pirate, blood dripping and everything.

'How come you get to keep it?' I ask.

'I earned it!' she says. 'All the years I worked for that old pirate! Every day in trying to pay off my debt, she'd charge me more and every day my debt got bigger not smaller. I tried not eating a thing, and working till I dropped but I still couldn't get ahead. She'd jus' charge me fare from one place to another, or say I broke something and charge me for fixing it. Right now she's figuring what it cost her to repair the rudder that she chopped off to get rid of me, and sharpen the axe what blunted chopping off my finger. What she calls working for her was jus' me slaving with money involved.'

'We don't use money where I'm from,' I say. 'And we don't have no slaves.'

'Good!' Saleesi says. 'That's where I'm going then. Money is stupid. Too hard to earn. Too easy to steal. Better off without it. And ain't one person better than another. Everyone's got a right to live free.' She puts her hands on her hips and stands legs apart in front of the wheel like she's a pirate queen.

'This is why we gotta rescue my friend Jaguar,' I tell her. I'm sure she'll understand now. 'He's paying off a debt for me, and it ain't fair. He done nothing wrong. He'd never do nothing wrong, and that's why they took him, coz it was easier than taking me.'

'Well, that ain't fair,' Saleesi says. 'We'll free him and we'll all go back to where you're from where there's no money and people is jus' fisherpeople, and we'll all live happily ever after.'

I smile. I think I like Saleesi.

'Where's your people from?' I ask.

'I don't hardly know,' she says. 'I was only eight when my father's boat was attacked by thieves and he hid me below. Pirate Bradshaw arrived after, and she said she was owed for answering his SOS message, so I gotta work it off. I din't have no one to stick up for me, coz my father disappeared that day, so I jus' ended up doing her pirating. Now I seen how she operates, I reckon it's her what owes me! You was lucky you set your croc on her.'

'That stupid croc!' I say. 'The only thing he ever learned was how to jump into boats! He was so stupid he got his legs caught in my net and dragged out to sea with me when I went chasing after my friend. I jus' fed him so as not to be cruel to a trapped animal. Now he thinks my net is his own personal sea-going beach. When we get to Valley of the Sun, maybe he'll get off there and look for some new territory for himself.'

Saleesi laughs. 'Ain't no place for crocs on Valley of the Sun. Best we leave him sitting right there, if he'll stay. Ain't no one gonna steal this little black boat if there's a big ol' croc sitting on it.'

VALLEY OF THE SUN

It's nearly evening when other boats sailing the same way as us appear out of the salt spray, then get close enough that my spyglasses let me pick out people going about their business on board. Most of them seem to be carrying salvage and fish. I adjust my next tack so we're going on a parallel path to them, and then we all sail into a sea fog so sudden, so wet and cold and thick, it gives me a fright like it slapped me. I ding the bell and wake Saleesi from her snoozing on the seat. 'Oh,' she says, stretching and yawning. 'You found it.'

'Found what?' I ask, coz I wasn't looking for no thick cold fog.

'Valley of the Sun,' she says.

'Nah,' I say, coz she's asleep and not seeing things proper. 'I jus' found a fog.'

'Sail on, you wormy-mouthed kid, and take another look,' she says, all bossy even though she's only a couple of years older than me tops.

So I do sail on, and I do take another look. The fog lifts suddenly and I'm under a clear sky and I've sailed through a ring of fog, a giant fog-ring made by little machines bobbing on the ocean. And right in the middle of the fog-ring sits something that makes my brain explode.

Boats, no, ships they're called when they're this huge. Mega ships, wide as islands, tall as mountains, lots of them sailing side by side, sides touching like they're welded together. I count five across the front. I count two deep on this side and two more behind them. All of them going in the same direction but stuck together firm as anything. Firmer even than *Licorice's* two hulls.

'Wow!' I say.

'Yep,' Saleesi says. 'That's the Valley of the Sun.'

'But that ain't no valley or island – that's a pile of giant ships stuck together.'

'A floating city. It controls all of the land on the

north-east of this continent. Jus' sails up and down, making sure all the people is doing what they should. Can't sail out and attack a moving capital hidden in fog. Can't tear down its sea walls. Can't ever guess how close or far away they is if you're up to something naughty. It's the best capital.'

Way, way up on the floating mega ships, there's buildings with lights on, there's even trees growing, reaching up for the sky, rising and falling, all of it together on the wide sea.

'Come on then, there's pontoons on the leeward side. Let's tie off and get aboard and find your friend. This low light will help.'

'Is boarding illegal?' I ask, coz I don't wanna get into worse trouble and have Jag paying for more.

'I dunno, do I? I've only been here pirating. Everything I did was illegal. That's what pirates do.'

'So will they arrest you here?' I ask.

'Nah, look at us. Two scruffy kids. They won't much care at all about us. It's that old Pirate Bradshaw they'll be wanting for thievery and selling stolen goods, not me. Plenty of scruffy beggar kids on Valley of the Sun.'

We tie off on a floating pontoon on the side of one of the large ships. The whole thing is moving forward very slowly, silently along with the ship. Saleesi leaps off and strides along the pontoon like she could walk across the ocean.

I jump off and stumble after her. First the pontoon drops away leaving my next footfall missing, and then it's running up to meet me. I drop to my knees and hang on and Saleesi laughs. She comes back and grabs my arm with her good hand and tows me past Uncle Croc, who seems to be sleeping, the gash on his head already dark and dry, up the jetty, up a rope ladder to another jetty, and up another ladder to an opening halfway up the hull of the mega ship. To the man with a sun crown waiting there she says, 'Anyone go near our boat and that trained croc will eat them!'

He yells at her in that strange language and blocks the way.

'I ain't got nothing,' she says and holds her hands out, palms up and nudges me with her elbow. 'Show him your hands, he thinks you been thieving.'

I show him my palms too. Then Saleesi kicks him in the shin and shoves me past him and into the ship.

The man yells and swipes at us but we're too fast and take off running. I check over my shoulder, and he's jus' grouching and frowning at us, and not chasing.

'He jus' thinks we're hanging around down here begging or looking for stuff to steal,' Saleesi says, slowing down to a quick walk. 'He won't bother chasing us, too many real thieves to keep his eye on,' which gives me hope that scruffy kids can come and go without a problem at all.

SOME KIND OF MAGIC

Saleesi tows me along into the dark of the inner ship, past electric engines and equipment and locked doors, then into a noisy corridor of stalls selling all manner of food and clothing and bits of equipment for boats and bits and pieces that look like some of the best salvage ever found. The smells is amazing! Fried food, and sweet food! My stomach growls.

Saleesi stops for a minute and digs into a pouch on her belt and pulls out a coin. She trades it for two paper bags and hands one to me. 'Fried prawn dumplings,' she says like I might know what that is.

The bag is greasy, and when I shove one little

wrapped pastry thing into my mouth, it's the best food I've ever had. Salty and crunchy on the outside, warm sweet prawn in the middle.

'Mmm. Mmm,' I say, coz I can't even speak!

Then Saleesi pulls me to a hallway full of tiny rooms and there's people waiting to get in the tiny rooms but I don't know what for, coz when the doors slide open on one of them it's jus' full of people trying to get out.

'Come on,' she says and drags me into the tiny room people is getting into until we're all packed in there, really close, and I can see why everyone wanted to get out. But music is playing in there, not a guitar, which is the only music I ever heard, but light and tinkly, and as soon as the doors close the sea lurches the boat straight up in a weird way. The doors open and everything is changed, there's all new shops here, and different walls. I go to get out and Saleesi grabs me and says, 'Nup, we're going to the top.'

'What d'ya mean?' I ask.

'This lift goes to the top deck. I wanna show you something.'

'This is a lift? I never been in a lift.' I heard of these from salvaging in the tall buildings, but those ones is long past working.

Saleesi laughs at me again in that way that makes me feel stupid and annoyed.

The doors open and close six or seven more times, all the time people getting off and on like they know where they're going in this place, even though I'm worrying I might not ever find *Licorice Stix* again.

Lots of people have the headbands on with the sun, and I eye them like they might be the ones who took Jag, but I don't think they is.

Saleesi grabs me and tows me out into a room with solid metal doors with portholes in them. She runs to one and pushes it open with her shoulder. We step out into the wet salt breeze onto a painted metal floor outside. The floor is bubbled with rust like my old bus, but painted over. She drags me to the rail, leans over, throws her hand open and says, 'Ta daa! The Valley of the Sun!'

Down below us, in the rectangle formed by all these giant ships, is a valley. A valley of green, shaped like an upside-down pyramid, all the terraces planted with crops and trees. Pretty shades of green and gold in lines and rows, all in steps down and down, to a point at the centre. And at that point right in the bottom, right in the centre, is a single common old mangrove tree.

Ha! Mangroves is the happiest trees in the inland sea. But even mangroves like for the salt water to be a little diluted. And all the other plants, the yellow wheat steps, the banana trees, they don't like salt water at all.

'Where do they get the water for all this?' I ask.

'Desal plant on one of the ships,' Saleesi says.

'Huh?' I ask.

'Takes the salt right out of the sea and jus' leaves the water. And it's all powered by these.' She hammers on the roof over the deck. 'Solar,' she says. 'And right up the top of the tallest part of the ships, wind. And under the sea, current turbines. With this garden and fish from the sea, Valley of the Sun don't need a thing from the land, and it won't never be drowned like other cities, not unless there's a storm bigger than what we already seen.'

I nod. 'There's been some monster big storms.'

Saleesi looks around. 'So where might your friend Jag be?'

'He was taken by the people with the suns on their heads who came to install tech on poles in the villages.'

Saleesi thinks for a moment. 'So an engineering family then,' she says, and points to a ship a long way across the valley. 'The engineers live there.'

She heads off across the deck at a jog, holding her missing finger hand close to her chest.

I follow her through a lot of people standing around talking, so many, so loud, I don't know how they're hearing each other, and the music is thumping like it's trying to be heard, and some of them is scruffy and smelling of sweat, and some of them is in better clothes.

We go through an area full of tables and chairs with people dining, all of them wearing fine clothes, some that sparkle like the stars. And the smells. Fried food, and sweet food, and my belly grumbles, like it's saying, *Remember me? Get me some prawn dumplings, right now!*

Up on a stage someone is twirling burning sticks and flashing knives in a way that looks too dangerous for anyone to be near. I slow to look and Saleesi grabs me.

'You can't stop here, dressed in rags and stinking like fish,' she says, and while I'm looking down at my clothes that do their job and keep the sun off me jus' fine, she says, 'Keep moving like you know where you're going and everyone will think you'll soon be someone else's problem and they won't stop you.'

I follow Saleesi, so glad for her and her knowledge about the Valley of the Sun. We run along decks and gangplanks and rope bridges and boardwalks, none of them quite as rolly as the floating pontoon we tied off on. We pass rich people and poor people, so many people, and stalls selling all manner of salvage and newly fashioned items, and grubby marketplaces and fancy eating squares and go down below to corridors and back up top, the sight of the green valley making me gasp and tingle all over again.

What a thing! What a thing to be at sea, surrounded by all this rolling ocean. I know Saleesi has explained it but it still seems to me to be some kind of magic. Imagine if we had this much garden back at Cottage Hill.

FOUND

When we reach the ship for the engineers, a man stands in our way guarding the boardwalk.

He asks us something in Valley of the Sun speak.

'This girl has important business here,' Saleesi says, bold as anything. 'Step aside.'

The guard switches to speak in my language. 'Important business with who?' he asks. 'Or are you just here to see what you can lift with your little light fingers?' Then he reaches out and slaps Saleesi on the side of the head like she's a dog what's been naughty. 'Get off with ya!' he says.

'No!' I yell. 'I am here to see Gerra. I have important information about the death of her sister.'

The guard looks at me and tilts his head. 'Where are you from, short stuff?'

'The Ockery Islands where her sister died.'

'I heard about that,' he says. 'A bad business. Go straight down to level two. Any detours, any pilfering, and I'll have you thrown in the lockup.'

'I won't,' I promise, even though I'm not sure what detours or pilfering is. Saleesi grabs my arm and tugs me across the gangway and we're onto the deck of the engineering families' ship. 'Great story!' she whispers.

'It's no story,' I say. 'Someone at Jacob's Reach pushed Gerra and her sister onto the rocks and then tried to cover it up. I ain't told no one, coz I need to find out more. These Valley of the Sun people seem to like blaming the wrong people for no good reason.'

'Ha!' Saleesi says. 'You's right about that.'

'Everyone on this ship has the same job?' I ask.

'Some do engines, some do welding, some do electronics, some do energy, but if you're born into an engineering family you jus' learn whatever they do.'

'But what if you're born in this ship and you're terrible at engineering and you want to grow vegetables or jus' go fishing?'

Saleesi laughs. 'Then you're a disappointment to your family and you move ships. Come on, I reckon he'll be down selling parts in the market.'

We take a lift down to level five, along with a man carrying a huge bag rattling with bits of metal, with pipes and wires sticking out and stabbing me as he leans forward to push some buttons.

The doors open into a large workroom. We squeeze past the man and wander around lots of tables with equipment for sale, and people behind those tables working with screwdrivers and wires and little machines that melt metal to stick wires to things. It's all very complicated, but it's the kind of thing Jag would like. I can't help wondering if he wants to be rescued from all this. There's two large corridors off the big room, and coz we can't see Jag anywhere here we start down one.

First there's little rooms with shelves all around and bowls and boxes on the shelves. One room is jus' small coils of wire, the next room silver and gold bits and bobs, and another room jus' has bowls of screws. I'm thinking if Jag is here, he'd have a full belt of useless junk by now. A kid in that room is sorting a tray of screws into the bowls by size and she turns and scowls at us. We duck on to the next room.

This room has two tables with kids around them taking apart bits of equipment. The bigger the kid, the bigger the bit of equipment they take apart. They're straining and grunting and sweating to chip away at rust, make old machinery into parts, heads down, tongues out, and then one looks up and right at me. Those dark eyes far apart on his round face looking so calm even when he's not. That scruffy hair, sun-bleached on the ends. That rattle of a belt of useful things as he stands up. It's Jag!

'I found you!' I say.

BACK TO LICORICE

Jag drops a spanner on the table. 'Neoma?' he says like he can't believe it.

'This one?' Saleesi asks, and grabs him with her good hand like he's jus' a spare part we need to pluck off the shelf and get out of here.

'Who is you?' Jag asks, pushing her hand off.

Saleesi don't answer, and she don't let go, she jus' drags him around the table to the door.

'This is my friend Saleesi and she's a pirate and we're rescuing you,' I tell him.

'Ex-pirate,' Saleesi says.

Jag's shaking his head, eyes wide like there's a problem.

'You don't wanna come home?' I ask. I blink sudden tears. Has he forgotten all our plans to be the best fisher team, the best salvage team ever? Does he jus' want to be an engineer now?

'I do!' he says. 'But you heard them, I gotta pay your fine or you or Da will be taken instead.'

'They won't come chasing across the sea after you again. I pulled out a wire, they put it back. Jus' how many wires and bolts you collected for them since then? I reckon you paid off my measly debt already.'

'But what if they catch us?' he asks.

'Jag, you wasn't so cautious about getting in here. I reckon you gotta be a bit daring to get out. And a bit quicker.' I pull him by his shirt, but he still ain't coming.

'I been learning so much here, Neoma. Stuff that can help us back at Cottage Hill. Cleaning up old metal, welding bits together, connecting wires—'

'Boy, they charging you room and food while you're working off this debt?' Saleesi asks like she's some ol' grown-up lady, even though she's jus' a head taller than us.

Jag nods.

'Then you ain't never gonna be able to afford to leave here,' she says. 'You may as well run now or live out your life here like these other kids from poor families.'

Jag looks at her and looks at me and looks at the other kids.

'Jag,' I plead. 'We've seen how this works. If you don't come with us now, you could never make it back home.' Then he runs out the door like he knows the fastest way out of here.

'Hey!' a teenager shouts. 'It's not break time! I'll report you!' He starts after Jag, but Saleesi runs and shoves the teenager into the room full of gold and silver bits. The rattling of lots of bits of metal and a girl yelling follows us down the hallway.

We chase after Jag and reach him as he's hauling open a heavy door. 'We'll take the stairs,' he says, and holds the door for us.

We leap over an old lady sleeping on a blanket on the floor. I turn back to check if she's alive and she's blinking faded blue eyes at me.

'Sorry, Aunty Susan,' Jag says, following us.

We're heading up the stairs, but Jag's pulling a coin from his pocket and he bends down, shoves it in Aunty Susan's bony hand and starts down the stairs. 'We can't get out that way, there's guards on top decks. We gotta go down to midships, take a gantry.'

'Great idea,' Saleesi says, like she understands that

ship-speak, and we both jump over Susan again, and call, 'Sorry, Aunty Susan!'

We charge down the stairs, leaping two at a time.

'Why's that old lady sleeping on the floor?' I ask. I thought she was dead.

'Susan used to work in parts too, but her hands got old and curled in and it hurt too much to keep working. She don't got no family except those she used to work with, so they let her sleep in the stairwell and give her food when they can. I don't got no family here either, and though I only got a da back home, at least I got a village what won't never treat me like that when I'm old. I've missed Cottage Hill so much, Neoma!'

'And we missed you,' I say, even though I been away as long as he has.

'Quit yer gabbing,' Saleesi says. 'Save your breath for running or we'll all wind up like Susan. We gotta get back to *Licorice Stix* real quick.'

WE GOTTA MOVE

Jag pushes open a door on level fifteen and we're in a
room full of pipes and greasy machinery.

'In here!' he whispers, and pulls us into a gap in
the piping and pushes us behind a large metal tank until
we're wedged against a wall in the dark. 'It's a secret
shortcut.'

A group of people go past and he pulls us out again,
and we run along a metal walkway that twists and turns
in and out of the machinery, and there's light ahead.
A hatch in the wall. Jag leads us out onto a gangway
that runs along the outside of the ship. It's shady out
here, and the smell of grease mixes with the smell of salt

and above us is the top edge of the valley, and greenery and trees. Far above that the last of the light is leaving the sky.

Soon we're on the next ship over and heading upstairs again to get to the deck and we keep running and ducking across decks and gangplanks to the next ship, and the next area, heading out to the far side of the ships where we left *Licorice*.

Saleesi takes the lead again, guiding us into and out of markets full of stalls so fast we're left dodging round people to keep up with her. She's jus' a flash of faded blue shirt tail between the busy hips and legs of overly tall people. And me, I'm watching her and looking back to make sure Jag is keeping up with me. Stuck in the middle, head flicking back and forth, and finally it happens. No blue shirt tail. But we gotta keep going, in the direction I think and hope is the right way.

We pass through a fancy restaurant and I remember what Saleesi said. Look like you're going somewhere, and no one will stop you. So I pick my head up and look at the far end of the restaurant, and stride quickly through like I'm going somewhere. A hand shoots out from a table and grabs me by the shirt, pulls me in so fast I lose my footing, and I'm face to face with Gerra!

'Let me go!' I say and fling myself away. Jag has very smartly ducked behind a crowd of people who is standing nearby talking so he won't be seen. He's peeking out.

Gerra hauls me back to face her. I give her an eyeballing, this woman I was gonna make a friend of by sticking to like a tick. This woman who don't speak my language but thinks I'm not to be trusted. This woman who knows I don't belong here. She's got a walking stick beside her, and she grabs it with her other hand and stands up so she's towering over me, and her gold headband glints in the hanging lights of the restaurant.

'We was nice to you,' I say, and my anger's boiling up in me like one of Ma's thunderheads.

Saleesi arrives waving her big knife and yelling in that Valley of the Sun language. And Jag steps out from around the people, who've all backed away from Saleesi.

Saleesi looks like she wants to slash Gerra.

'No!' I tell Saleesi, and put my body between them.

'Put your knife away.'

Saleesi grumbles and sticks the cutlass back in her belt.

Guards run through another part of the restaurant, heading somewhere, looking around. Jag gasps and ducks. Gerra looks over at them too, and when I spect her to lift her hand and wave and call out, she sits back down on the chair and looks from Jag to me.

'Tell her we din't have nothing to do with her sister's death,' I say.

Saleesi tells her.

'Tell her she has to remember how it happened or the wrong people is gonna take the blame,' I say.

Saleesi does.

'She got knocked onto the rocks near the jetty at Jacob's Reach, but they din't mean for her sister to die. Ask her does she remember the trees that got cut down? The trees with symbols on them?'

Saleesi says it, and I lean over the table and dip my finger in the dark sauce on Gerra's plate and draw on her fine white table cover the zigzag I seen on the cut-down tree, MW. 'M for Aunty Meryn,' I say.

Gerra stares. Then she nods, pushes me off, and says some of her words. I grab Jag's hand and we run.

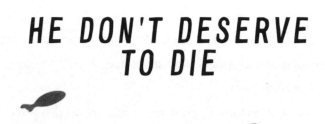

HE DON'T DESERVE
TO DIE

We follow Saleesi winding and ducking through laneways and market stalls and piles of rubbish and poor people begging. Finally we's heading down swaying gangplanks to the pontoons where we left *Licorice*.

There's noise down there, on the pontoons, shouting, feet on boards, shapes of people running along the pontoons. Solar lanterns swing from poles lighting everything in a swaying moving light, so dark shapes of people is lit up, and then the rolling sea, and then shapes again. Torches flash across *Licorice* and Uncle Croc is in those light flashes, his jaws wide and snapping at people trying to board.

I grab Saleesi. 'We have to swim in from the other side!' I tell her.

We all look at the dark water below. It's a drop from this gangway down into a gap between pontoons far below, not as far as my last jump, maybe only a couple of floors of an old tower block, and then a swim under the floating pontoons, and then under Uncle Croc and *Licorice's* hulls.

'Sharks,' Saleesi says, and her face is pale in the weak light, and why wouldn't it be, she's tussled with the biggest of sharks.

'Sharks and that croc,' Jag says, and of course he ain't going in the night water out on the wide sea, not with his fear of sharks and crocs.

Me then, only I can do the swim, but how do I get Jag and Saleesi to the boat? Out in the night there's a pontoon with swinging lanterns, further up the hull of this mega ship. Those lanterns is going up and down so much, showing that the pontoon's too rough for boats to tie off to. It's catching much more of the swell than back here. If I could get Licorice going, I can do a sweep past that wild pontoon. Slow enough so maybe I could pick them up. I point. 'Reckon you can hang on to that until I get *Licorice* there?' I ask.

Saleesi with her most excellent sea legs nods.

Jag jus' croaks, 'Uhh . . .'

I don't wait for his yes. I climb between the ropes of the gangway and leap into the dark.

Down I go. Warm wet night air whistling past my ears. *Slap!* Hard water stings my shins where they're hauled into my body and I'm sinking down and the rolling wave slams me at the hull, rough and scrapey with rust and barnacles. I din't think the water would be swirling this way on the landward side of the ship. I kick hard to the surface, grab a lungful of air and get wiped across the hull again. This hull is moving, not fast but faster than it seemed from above. Fast enough to suck me under, churn me through a motor and spit me out the back?

I hope not!

I put my feet against it and push off hard, swim flat out, and break the suction of the ship. Then I have to dive under a pontoon and up the other side. Light flashes over me and I worry that people will see me, but I'm jus' a dark wet head in a dark wet sea and no one cries out. I dive under another pontoon. Waves roll and crash into my mouth jus' when I think it's safe to take a breath, then push me back against the pontoon. I don't know that I'm a strong enough swimmer to get to *Licorice*, now I'm here. Ma's always saying I bite off more than I can chew, and maybe this bite is too big for me.

I push off the pontoon, swim hard, duck under another roll that pushes me back. I'm getting nowhere. But I take a breath and keep trying. Eventually *Licorice* will come to me. She's being towed along by the ship's pontoon, and the whole Valley of the Sun moving slowly along.

I'm small and light and I'm a good floater. I think people who float good forget how hard it is for people who don't float to swim. Jag don't float. He sinks. When he goes in the sea he has to thrash around jus' to stay afloat. Me, I jus' cycle my legs slowly or lie on my back and flutter my hands. Swimming is easy for me. This is why it's me in the water, swimming to save my two friends, and I can't let them down. Jus' like Saleesi will swing that big knife for me, or Jag would be taken so far away for me, I can't let them down. I pull with my arms and kick with my legs and try to figure out the swell. I take a breath, duck and swim under the pontoon where all the noise is coming from, the feet slapping and the shouting.

Most of it's in Valley of the Sun language, but then a man screams and says in my language, 'I ain't trying again! It tried to take my arm off!'

'Fetch a gun. We'll have to shoot it,' someone else says.

I'm kinda responsible for Uncle Croc. He wasn't to know better when he boarded in his cove, and he's had to deal with a trappy net, an old pirate and a shark. It's not his fault he does croc things. He don't deserve to die for it.

CHASE US ACROSS THE WATER

I'm glad for the shouting and stomping up on the pontoon. Neither the people nor Uncle Croc notices when I swim right under *Licorice Stix* and slide up onto her deck from the back. I catch my breath and cast off the rope. It was a good rope and I'm sad to leave it on the pontoon.

Licorice drifts out, and by the time the people on the pontoon figure out she's not tied anymore it's too far for them to jump, not that jumping is a good idea with a snapping croc on board.

I crank the sail and get *Licorice* moving out to sea, putting in some distance to make them give up chasing her along pontoons. As I swing her about to come back to the pontoon further up, a shout comes bouncing across the water.

'There's the boy!'

The engineering people is looking for him!

'No!' I yell. 'That's our boy. That boy is a boy of Cottage Hill and I'm taking him back!'

I pull the sails tighter and get *Licorice* skipping across the rolling sea. She hits the tops of the swell and slows then speeds, creaking and groaning like she'd rather be fishing.

The pontoon where Saleesi and Jag wait is heaving in the swell. Waves are swamping over it and the lights are swinging wildly. Starting along it in the swooping light is dark shapes, their steps wonky and staggering. More shouting.

'You there! Come here!'

It's not for sure they'll even get to Jag and Saleesi with all that staggering, but anybody can drop to their hands and knees and crawl.

'Jump!' I yell. 'Swim!' But they won't be going into that dark sea, neither of them. The shapes get closer and closer to them, and *Licorice* can't close the gap fast enough. All this for nothing?

Saleesi backs up almost into the people wobbling down the pontoon and runs and leaps into the dark sea ahead of me, so sure that I can get to her, and then Jag follows! He's not even ditched his belt with all the tools on!

I pull out a life ring on a rope and throw it out into the dark in their direction, screaming, 'Grab a hold!' Then I winch the boom to turn the sail about. In that turning time, that moment of slowness, if they can grab the ring then, I can winch them in.

But it's dark out there. Light glints off water. Is it a head? I don't know.

'Do you have it?' I yell into the dark. I can't winch in before they both have it. Then *Licorice's* hull bumps, lifts, and slides over something big. A fin cuts the water beside her in the swinging light from the pontoon. Uncle Croc crawls hard up against one hull, a rock invisible.

'Grab the ring! I'm hauling it in!' I scream, and wrap the rope around the winch.

I get it cranking as *Licorice* picks up speed again, making the winch grind and groan.

Behind me in a flash of light there's a head and a shirt on the life ring. Let it be two people! Don't let me leave one of them behind! How, though? How will Jag with his heavy tool belt and his knack for sinking, how will he grab anything? And what if the shark gets to them? Has she been trailing *Licorice Stix*, still upset about losing her croc meal and her pirate girl meal?

The life ring hits the back of the boat with a thud and flips up over the edge and onto the deck. I shut off the winch and run to the back of the boat.

Saleesi is there, clinging to the ladder, her shaved head round and shiny with water in the moonlight.

'Saleesi!' I scream. 'We have to go back for Jag!'

Something rattles on the ladder, and Saleesi grunts. She's hauling on a belt full of tools and it's Jag, bent double, coughing and gasping.

I lean over and pull him up by the belt too and soon he's lying on the deck, spewing water. Saleesi crawls in herself, spitting away the salt.

'I'm sorry I pulled you in so quick,' I say, 'the shark is back!'

A yell carries across the water and the pontoon behind us lifts in the pools of light and drops and there's splashes as people crash into the sea.

'I think she's busy right now,' Saleesi says. 'Let's get out of here!'

I pull the sails tight again, trying to get away from the screams that bounce off giant hulls and the sea surface and chase us across the water.

'So you got a trained croc *and* a trained shark?' Saleesi asks.

'No way!' I say. 'They's jus' doing what they do. And they're unnaturally attracted to this boat!'

'Well, I hope she gets fed, is all I can say!' Saleesi says, which is a really horrible thing to think.

I feel guilty that the shark might bite someone, but that's stupid. She's not my shark. She'd jus' as soon eat me if she could.

FALLEN IN WITH A PIRATE GIRL

Licorice Stix catches the wind and I put up the jib and we're soon skimming away, thumping the swell. I tell Jag all about our adventures at sea with the pirate and the croc and the shark and how we'll soon be home.

I wind the jib sail half down so we're sailing using the onshore breeze to keep going through the night. I turn the wheel over to Jag and point out the pointers and the Southern Cross. Jag says he can't sleep coz he don't trust that the croc can't climb up over the hull and slide onto the deck beside us.

I sleep top deck on one seat, and Saleesi says she's going to sleep down in the hull.

'How come you fallen in with a pirate girl?' Jag asks, jus' when my eyes get heavy.

'She din't want to be no pirate,' I say. 'She wants to leave that life behind and be a fishergirl like me.'

'That's what she tol' you. How you know she's not planning to steal *Licorice Stix*?'

'Coz she coulda lost me and stole her ten times over already,' I say. 'She came back for us on the Valley of the Sun and she saved you, so yeah, I trust her. I been careful, Jag. You don't have to trust her, but you can trust my feelings about her.'

I turn over. Jag being cautious is sometimes a pain.

READY TO BATTLE

I'm woken by the cranking whirr of Jag flat out winding the torch. The torch splutters a weak light that sets dots floating in front of my eyes.

'Someone's following us!' he says.

I'm on my feet, blinking into the dark, my head swirling with the dream I jus' had that I was fishing and pulling up shark babies that were wailing like real babies for their mama. 'Tack and hoist the jib sail full!' I say. 'Don't shine a light to show where we are!'

In my sleep head, I can't help thinking that the wailing baby sharks has brought the mama shark down on us.

I crank the winch to bring the boom around for a tack. Then the wailing starts for real. Or did it jus' get louder?

Jag gets the light swinging around to where the wailing's coming from. It passes over a glint of metal and a head in the sea.

Jag swings the torch back, and it's the wet shaggy head of Pirate Bradshaw, knife clenched between her brown teeth, wailing like ten thousand night birds, arms outstretched, the swell lifting her up to grab on to the back of our boat. Behind her there's the sound of sails collapsing. That *waloompf* sound heavy canvas makes, and the faint whiteness of the hull of the pirate's yacht.

I gasp so hard I almost swallow my tongue. Jag whimpers and drops the torch. It rolls around shining on a flat bare foot landing on the deck and a rush of water dripping off clothes.

I release the boom and pull the wheel to swing the boom across the deck, hoping to knock her off.

Jag's too busy backing across the deck to see what I'm doing, so I tackle him to the floor, and when the torch rolls around again, the old pirate hag is gone. But there wasn't a splash. There wasn't an angry wail. I don't think she's gone back in the sea.

When the boom swings back, she's clinging to it, hands and feet, like an upside-down possum.

'Now, now,' she says. 'No need to be like that.' She drops to the deck. I leap to my feet, and I'm looking around for Saleesi in the rolling torchlight. Where is she? How do we get rid of this old pirate?

Jag and I back around the wheel and the pirate follows.

'You took my salvage,' she says. 'I reckon you owe me a debt.'

'This ain't salvage. This is my boat,' I say.

'A kid can't own a boat. I jus' lost me a good deckhand. I reckon it's gonna take two to replace her.'

'Tell her,' Jag whispers, maybe thinking we can trade Saleesi for our own lives.

'Tell me what?' the pirate asks.

'If you don't get off right now, I'll set my croc on you,' is what I tell her.

The pirate flicks the torch up with her bare foot into her other hand and shines it over to the net.

As the light slides over the hull, a hand picking up a coil of rope is lit up and then vanishes. Saleesi!

The croc's eyes glow in the light. He's squashed hard up against the hull, pretending to be a log once more.

'Grab on to something!' I say to Jag. We both grab the wheel.

And I wait for that bump against the hull of *Licorice* that might be the shark, but it doesn't come.

'That bony stretch of leather don't scare me,' the pirate says. 'Now, let's see. You stole my salvage, and sunk my other salvage, it's two years' work you owe me.'

'It ain't salvage, it's thieving!' I say. 'Salvage is when you take stuff no one else owns!'

She spins the torch on my face and pulls out a rope. Before I know it, she's looped Jag's wrist to the wheel, the torch now in her teeth and that knife at my nose to stop me from moving. I'm imagining spectacular moves where I get the knife and free Jag and do bad things to her with it. Me who hates killing fish! But in the light of the torch it seems she's already bleeding from under her hair, dark red lines running down and mixing with the sea water on her wrinkly face. She gets Jag's other wrist tied to the wheel, reaches up and wipes the blood from her face and stares at her fingers, rubs them together and twists them to catch the light. It's red alright. Even smells like blood.

'Did you get bit?' I ask.

Then two feet land squarely on the old pirate's shoulders, knocking her to the deck, me leaping away from that falling knife. Saleesi appears out of nowhere.

I dive for the knife, but the pirate pushes me off and stands up with it in her hand. The torch rolls across the deck.

Saleesi, who's tied herself to the mast by a rope around her waist, is on her feet facing the pirate. Her with the pirate's big knife, and the pirate with the smaller one, looking like they're ready to battle.

'You!' the pirate shouts. 'You owe me a rudder.'

'A rudder, Pirate Bradshaw?' Saleesi says, and slides her cutlass away into her belt. 'I got you a rudder, a whole boat, two crew and a decent croc dinner to boot. I reckon me and you is square.'

'I tol' you!' Jag says to me, wrestling with the rope around his wrist.

A FAIR FIGHT

I'm staring at the dark outline that's Saleesi, trying to read her face. I don't think she wants a truce with Pirate Bradshaw, but I can't see her face to tell me if she's telling the truth or not.

'I tol' you!' Jag says again. 'Can't trust a pirate!'

'Saleesi?' I ask.

Pirate Bradshaw don't put away her knife. 'Well then, I'm sorry about throwing you to the sharks. Seems I was hasty in judging your character.'

'Sharks!' Saleesi says, and spits on the deck. 'All tiny out there. I ate a couple for my dinner while I was swimming after this boat.'

'It's jus' you din't seem to be bringing this zippy little catamaran that'd fetch a fair price back to me, my lovey,' the old pirate says, and smiles, brown teeth wet in the torchlight.

I swallow. I know that quiet pause when a lie runs out of wind. I know it too well.

Then Jag does this amazing jump where he flips and lands on his feet on the other side of the wheel. He pulls the wheel down hard with him, which sets the boom swinging back, flying through the dark at these two pirates facing off.

Jus' before the boom hits, Saleesi leaps into the air away from it, and it catches her and takes her away. It knocks Pirate Bradshaw into the seat so hard she slides to the deck and this time the knife slides further from her.

I grab it and saw-cut Jag free, but the pirate's coming at me again. Her eyes is little torchlights and she pulls an even smaller knife from her pocket and I dunno how long she can keep up this game of knives. If I take twenty knives from her, will she still be standing there with a needle-sized knife ready to battle? I believe Saleesi now when she said no one can kill this old pirate.

Me and Jag scramble across the cockpit, and I can't see where Saleesi's gone to in the torchlight pointing across the deck. I lift my bigger knife.

There's a splash off the back of the boat and then *Licorice* lurches. The pirate don't even need to grab on. She's so used to the lurching sea that the nudging of giant sharks is nothing. She keeps taking steps towards us.

I pull Jag behind me. I only jus' got him back, and I promised him a going-home. Ain't no one taking him or me.

The old sea hag is almost on us and there ain't nowhere to go. The shark is waiting for us overboard, the croc is on the trapeze net. Will we have to be slaves to a pirate now?

There's a rush of wind and a shape passes me in the dark. It's Saleesi swinging from the mast! She bowls into Pirate Bradshaw, sends her sailing overboard. There's a mighty splash and then Saleesi's sailing back at us. I leap up and grab her feet. Get dragged across the deck as I bring her to a stop.

Then she drops out of the rope and we run to the side and peer out into the dark. Jag arrives with the torch.

Saleesi is holding her hand to her chest. Her finger blood is all over her shirt, and the bandage I so carefully wound around her finger stump is tied off on *Licorice's* ladder and trailing out the back. That bloody bandage.

'You called the shark with your own blood?' I ask.

She nods. 'You're not the only one who can train a shark,' she says. There's a scream and a splash, and Saleesi grabs my arm. 'We should get out of here before she kills that shark and comes back for us.'

'Is you dreaming? D'ya see the size of that shark?' Jag asks. He's got the torchlight on the old mama shark's massive fin and thrashing tail as she swings around for another attack.

'Yep!' me and Saleesi say together.

'It's a fair fight, if I'm being honest,' Saleesi says. 'Much fairer than wrestling that poor croc.'

'She got took by a croc, and a shark?' Jag asks.

'Yep!' me and Saleesi say together and grab at the boom ropes, so we can get outta here.

THE LAST LITTLE BIT HOME

We run and get the boom winched off and *Licorice* moving, catching that onshore breeze to anywhere but here. Jag keeps cranking the torch and sweeping around the boat, checking for sharks and pirates and that the croc ain't moved, and after seeing that old Pirate Bradshaw surf in on the swell with her wild wail and that knife between her teeth, I don't think we can be too careful. I'm grateful for Jag being overcautious.

I locate the pointers on the horizon, the planet already turned too far from the Southern Cross, so I can keep *Licorice Stix* heading steadily south. All of us are too scared to stop.

The earth turns like it does, and soon enough the sun is on the horizon, so I throw out some lines coz we're all starving. We get four large fish in a rush, and I give two to the croc and fillet the other two for us, and throw Uncle Croc the skeletons. I'm out of coconut and lime, so I have to pull the little solar oven out of the other hull and tilt it at the morning sun.

While we're waiting for it to heat up, I find another bandage in the first-aid kit and keep Saleesi's raw-fish-picking hands away from our breakfast fish by bandaging up her finger stump again. She's given the end of her finger a beating, getting it to bleed all over Pirate Bradshaw and into the sea. Must've hurt something awful. Marta's gonna have to stitch it when we get back.

Soon the oven puts out cooked-fish smells and we sit and pick the fish apart with our fingers, me and Jag putting our raw bits back in for more cooking when we find them, Saleesi jus' swallowing hers down.

A full belly and skidding across the waves heading home makes me happy. Ain't no way no one is gonna catch us now. Soon we'll be back on the inland sea where Ma will skin me alive for taking her boat and letting a shark put a big old dent in the front.

Saleesi and Jag is both asleep when land comes into view, so I let them sleep on.

Uncle Croc lifts his head, waddles carefully to the front of the net and sniffs the air. 'Go on,' I say. 'Even with a hole in your head, you can swim that far.'

But coz he's a lazy croc that'd rather ride, or maybe he's afraid Mama Shark ain't got a belly full of pirate, he waits till we're closer, then he turns back to me and opens his mouth wide, like he's asking if there's any chance of another fish.

'Get off my boat,' I tell him. 'Right now!'

He shuts his mouth and slides into the sea. His tail swishes back and forth as he swims in to land. I hope he don't hop up on every boat now and spect a meal.

I sail down the coast to the sunken surf coast towers and then turn in and sail the inland sea the way we always do when we're heading home from salvaging.

Jag sits up yawning. 'Oh,' he says. 'I thought I might never see this place again.'

'We would always come to find you, Jag,' I say.

'And what if Valley of the Sun comes for me?' he asks.

'I gotta admit, that's a real problem. They promised to come back and find out who killed Gerra's sister. If Gerra can't remember proper, then we might be in deep.' Then

I tell him what the boy who helped me with the croc told me on top of the hill. 'Something happened after they cut down Aunty Meryn's tree,' I say.

Jag nods and we stare out at the Ockery Islands we know so well, the bays and fishing spots we'd named together. Fat Fish Bay. Sandy Channel. Snaggy Rock Gorge. Stumpy Point. Broken Tree Pass. Home.

This last little bit home seems like the longest part of the journey coz I know everyone is waiting back there to see what became of me and Jag and *Licorice Stix*, missing for so long, and coz even though I'll be facing a lot of shouting, at least I'll have fixed the problem I caused when I pulled the wires and got Jag taken.

LET'S GET HOME

'You should go talk to him. Make him tell you the whole story,' Saleesi says.

'What?' I ask.

'Well, a crime happened coz someone is dead and someone got hurt, and those Valley of the Sun sea dogs will come to make someone pay, so make sure they don't go blaming the wrong person, coz it might be someone from your place,' she says.

Jag nods. 'She's right.'

I shrug. 'Even if I could get him to talk, d'ya think Uncle Sorren or Ma will let me go out there to do it?'

Jag shades his eyes and looks to port and looks to starboard, then gives me one of his most excellent grins that's also a bit adventurous.

'Jag!' I say. 'Is you saying we jus' sail off there now?'

'We'll go around the back of the island and throw out some lines like they's crab pots,' Jag says.

'Well, look at you making plans for adventures!' I say, and elbow him.

Once we're anchored behind Jacob's Reach, Jag throws out lines and makes a show of sitting out on the boat waiting while Saleesi and I sneak ashore. I've described croc-boy to her real well. He's not up the hill talking to his cousin Lucy, so we split up.

I sneak to the edge of the village, and climb up a tall tree to spy. People hardly ever look up. They walk around looking where to put their feet, so sitting in a tree is an excellent place to spy.

People is tending the fire and loading up boats, and kids is running around laughing and yelling.

That man that might be croc-boy's da is still sitting outside the hut with the boarded-up windows and someone brings him some food, but no croc-boy.

Finally I give up and climb down and sneak back over the hill and head down the island to where *Licorice* and Jag is waiting. I'm creeping through the trees when Saleesi yells, 'I'll whomp you!'

I take off running towards her voice. Someone's growling, and sticks is cracking. And up against a tree is Saleesi, trying to hold down a struggling croc-boy. Beside him is a pile of sticks tied up in a belt.

'Get off me!' he shouts.

'Hey, stop shouting,' I say. 'We jus' wanna ask you some questions.'

'You!' he says. 'I don't have nothing to say.'

Saleesi pulls out her cutlass. 'I'm a pirate, you know,' she says. 'I can split your tongue for you like a lizard or you can tell us what we want to know.'

Croc-boy sticks his tongue out. 'Go on then!' he dares.

'You wormy-mouthed dog,' Saleesi says and grabs his tongue in her fist. Which makes him pull it in real quick.

'She is a pirate, you know,' I say. 'Today's her last day of pirating, and she's trying to not be so . . . err . . . piratey. She's gonna take up fishing.'

'Well, her hands taste like fish,' he says and spits. 'So she got that part right.'

'What's your name?' I ask.

'Echo,' he says.

'What, what, what?' Saleesi asks, and I thump her shoulder for it.

'Listen to me, Echo. We's all gentle Ockery Islands people, and these new Valley of the Sun people think Cottage Hill had something to do with the missing siblings. They's gonna take Marta or someone else to pay the debt. You gotta tell us what happened.'

'Not allowed to,' he says.

'Yeah, well, we's not allowed to be sneaking round here, trying to figure this out,' I say. 'But here we is, trying to save an innocent person from paying for something someone else done. Jus' tell us what happened and we can make sure the Valley of the Sun people don't overreact and come storming in here with guns to shoot people, like what they did at our place.'

'They did?' he asks. He looks from me to Saleesi like he's looking for the truth.

'Fifty of them, a hundred maybe,' Saleesi says.

'Let me go. Then I'll tell you,' the boy says.

'You mud-worm,' Saleesi says.

'Nah, he's a good guy,' I tell Saleesi. 'He knows things went badly wrong and a small crime turned into a big one real quick. And he knows it's better if the Valley of the Sun know that outright, no matter what Jacob or his da says. He don't want no one in his village getting shot at.'

Saleesi gets off him, stands up and puts her knife away. 'He hurt my finger,' she mutters, and gives me a dark look.

Echo stands up. 'I ain't s'posed to talk about it,' he says. 'But all we did was, we locked up one Valley of the Sun for what he did to Aunty Meryn's tree and the other two got so mad. They went down the jetty and got out weapons. And our guy was holding that log to show what those three did to his ma's grave, so he jus' ran at them to chase them back to their boat. He shouldn'ta done that. He was real mad about his ma's tree. They zapped him and he fell into them. He was already asleep when they fell on the rocks. We's not killers.'

'Who?' I ask. 'Who bashed them off the jetty?'

Echo dodges around Saleesi and runs. 'Not up to me to say!' he yells.

Saleesi throws up her hands. 'I ain't chasing him down again. He runs like he's got a jib out!'

'Won't have to,' I say. 'I think I know now. Let's get home!'

FETCH HIM BACK

We tack into the bay under Cottage Hill, and there's a
wail that starts way up at the shacks. And I wonder if
Pirate Bradshaw beat us here! But it's not her.

It's Ma, my own ma, running wildly down to the jetty
and jumping up and down there screaming,

'Neoma! Neoma!' like I can somehow get there faster.
I wish I could, my throat prickles like sobs is stacking up
in there.

'Jaguar!' she screams, and all the aunties and uncles
and old people and young cousins come running down
to the water's edge. 'Jaguar!' they yell. 'Neoma!' And I feel

mighty grand to be the one who's bringing home this son of the whole village.

I blink through fat squirmy tears but I can't see Jag's da anywhere.

'You din't tell me the people of Cottage Hill were so . . . bouncy,' Saleesi says.

Ma is on *Licorice Stix* like a flea on a dog even before we've touched the jetty, and she's hugging me and holding me out and yelling at me about what did I think I was doing and hugging me again and blubbing up a storm. She hugs Jag and passes him over onto the jetty where people is tying off *Licorice* for us. They pass him from person to person, hugging him, rubbing his hair, patting his back, and he's laughing as he's pushed from person to person like a toy.

Then Ma hands me over for the same treatment and grabs hold of Saleesi, wrapping her in big hugs, her eyes wide as scallop shells, but she too is pulled off the boat and people hug her like they knew her and lost her and got her back, same as us. The three of us is left standing in front of Marta. Ma comes and wraps her arms around me like I might slip away again if she lets go.

'Where's Da?' Jag asks, still looking around, frowning hard like maybe Uncle Sorren never woke up from that dart.

'He's gone to Valley of the Sun to fetch you back,' Marta says.

Me and Jag look at each other. I dunno how he'll find it, avoid pirates, and get past the Valley of the Sun people even if he does.

'But why?' I say. 'I already fetched him back.'

'Sorren went to fetch you back too,' Marta says.

'But who's gonna fetch him back?' I ask.

'He can fetch himself back,' Marta says.

I know she's wrong. But she don't listen when I tell her she's wrong, and Ma says to stop nagging Marta, and go wash that fish stink off while she fixes us some food. Is it any wonder I don't tell people what I'm up to?

Jag says not to worry, we got enough information to trade for his da back and if we have to steal *Licorice* and go back to Valley of the Sun again, we will. I dunno what's come over Jag lately. At this rate, I'll be the cautious one!

AN EXCELLENT IDEA

Three days go by with me and Jag sitting on the hill in the shade of the poles watching for that Valley of the Sun boat to come, hopefully bringing back Uncle Sorren. We's making plans to rescue him if we don't see him soon. Got rocks and bits of bark laid out in a map marking out the coastal towns and where we guess Valley of the Sun is.

When the spyglasses finally catch the twinkle of that gold sun shining on an approaching boat, I shove it into Jag's hands and hurtle down the hill screaming, 'Valley of the Sun! Valley of the Sun is coming!'

Saleesi joins me letting everyone know, banging on roofs with her cutlass, kicking up a row.

Jag stays up top to make sure his da's in the boat. Ma and Dizzy take our best fishing boats and hide them up the creek, jus' in case Valley of the Sun want payment for something. Everyone else hides the littlies for the same reason.

Marta puts on her best shirt and comes to the top of the jetty standing tall as she can. 'Neoma, go and hide like the others,' she says. 'We don't want to lose you. Let adults handle adult business.'

I nod, but Jag is tearing down the hill and the most excellent grin stretched across his face tells me his da is on board.

He jumps up and down when he gets to me. 'He's okay! He's okay!'

'Yay!' I say and jump up and down with him.

'Get on to somewhere you won't get taken again.' Marta waves her hands at us like we're noisy chooks.

'But Jag ain't seen his da for ages!' I say, and we don't get away, we hang close jus' ducking down behind some dinghies on the beach.

Ma and Dizzy get back about the same time as the Valley of the Sun arrives, and when Jag's da sets foot on the jetty, and ties the boat off for them, it's too much for Jag. 'He's home!' he whispers. Then he leaps out before I can grab him and runs flat out to the jetty!

Me and Saleesi jus' watch over top of a dinghy.

Three Valley of the Sun people have guns and the older woman with the hair that's black instead of grey is with them again. They help Gerra out of the boat too. Has she remembered? They hold Jag off when he tries to get to his da, and that makes me burning hot. I leap up to go running over there to yell and kick some shins or something but Saleesi tackles me and drags me back behind the dinghy. 'Don't be a numbat,' she says. 'Wait and see what they're here to do.'

What they do is stomp about waving the guns and shouting. They stomp right past Marta and Ma and Dizzy up to the empty village. They're dragging Jag's da around like they don't intend to let him go. Maybe they only come to take Jag back. Maybe Gerra still don't remember what really happened.

'We gotta go tell them what happened out at Jacob's Reach,' I say.

Saleesi shakes her head. 'Do they look like they're gonna listen to a scruffy kid right now?' she asks.

Gerra and the older woman are talking with Marta in that funny language they use. 'We told you we were coming back for answers!' the older woman shouts in our language.

Jag is up the hill clinging to his da, as the people with the guns drag them hut to hut in search of someone. Is it me they's looking for?

It don't look like anyone's gonna be sitting down over a cup of tea for a chat, so there's nothing for it. I sprint along the beach, then down the jetty, cast off the Valley of the Sun boat and leap into it. There's a thud beside me – it's Saleesi. 'Where we goin'?' she asks.

'Jacob's Reach,' I say.

'Ha!' she laughs and shoves the boat out from the jetty.

'Hey!' the older woman shouts.

Ma and Dizzy run down the jetty. 'Get back here, right now, Neoma!' Ma yells.

I wave and grin and keep going. We're already turning and hoisting the sail and there's no boat but Marta's old boat to chase us with, the bigger boats all hiding up the creek. This is an excellent idea.

Ma and Dizzy run to grab Marta's boat but Marta shouts, 'No! I'll take it.' Maybe Marta knows my plan.

The older woman yells and the three people with guns come running back down from the village with Jag and his da. All of them shouting at us.

Then all five of the Valley of the Sun people climb into Marta's boat, along with Jag and his da, and Marta. A boat that normally holds two or three sitting low and heavy in the water, with eight in it!

'Look at it!' Saleesi says and laughs. She stands on the stern, legs wide apart like a pirate, and screams, 'You'll sink, you wormy-brained dogs!'

I'm jus' happy they're all leaving Cottage Hill and following me to Jacob's Reach. That's where the trouble should be. With Jacob, who lied about what happened.

OCKERY ISLANDS CUSTOMS

Ma and Dizzy is sprinting back towards the creek, so they'll have *Licorice Stix* skimming the bay after us soon enough.

Across the risen sea we sail, working the Valley of the Sun boat as best we can. It's fitted out a bit different to what we're used to with seats and cushions and sunshades and all manner of beeping gadgets, but we've not got time to figure it out. We gotta get a good lead to stop Ma catching up and spoiling it all.

Black sails appear a long way behind and creep up on Marta's little boat with its white sail, and they pull alongside. Both sets of sails drop. I don't have spyglasses but I think there's people climbing onto *Licorice Stix*.

'They'll be after us soon in Licorice,' Saleesi says.

I nod. I'm thinking hard about what I'll say to Jacob. What I'll say to that old woman from Valley of the Sun when she catches up to me. How will I get them to listen? It's a long way to Jacob's Reach and it seems like both sets of sails behind us are hoisted again way too soon. *Licorice* is faster than most boats. She'll be on us like a tick.

Me and Saleesi work the sail, tacking back and forth across the inland sea, as the earth turns and puts the sun low in the sky, and finally Jacob's Reach is in view. *Licorice* is hot on our tail. We turn and tack and it feels like we're sailing right at them for a moment. They turn early and try to cut us off, but the tack slows them. It takes a moment for the sail to move across and refill. The people on the deck are slow pulling it tight. I think I know why. Only Marta, the old woman and two tall Valley of the Sun people are standing on the deck of *Licorice*. None of them as good sailors as Ma, Dizzy or Uncle Sorren, all left behind on Marta's boat.

'Ahoy!' Saleesi yells, cheeky as a galah. 'How's the fishing!'

'Shush!' I say. 'They got guns and they's already mad.'

'Drop your sail!' the old woman yells.

We don't. I guess a bit of Saleesi's pirating ways rubbed off on me when it comes to doing what I'm told.

Our lead on *Licorice Stix* gets smaller and smaller the closer we get to Jacob's Reach, and I'm wondering if all Jacob's people will see is the silly croc-girl getting told off in their bay and hauled back to Cottage Hill.

We sail fast up to Jacob's Reach's jetty coz I don't really care if we get a scrape on their tin boat. *Licorice* is so close someone will be leaping for the stern as I'm leaping off the bow. Saleesi drops all the sails and we coast up close to the poles. I leap for the deck with the tie off rope, wrap it around a pole and throw it back to Saleesi for her to deal with slowing the boat proper. Then I run up into the centre of Jacob's Reach. 'Hide! Hide! Valley of the Sun is here!' I yell.

People come out and stare. None of them laugh, coz they all know they done something wrong.

'Hide your littlies, they got guns!' I yell. Then parents get moving, and kids is rounded up, grabbed by parents and they run up into the forest and over the hill.

'What's going on!' Jacob shouts. He comes stomping down from a cottage, his face red and grumpy.

I point back to *Licorice Stix* tying off at their jetty. 'They came to our village, waving guns, and now they're on our boat,' I say. 'You gotta tell them what happened when their people came here. You gotta tell them so they don't blame us!'

Jacob glares at me. 'You're in their boat. You brought them here!'

'Yeah,' I say. 'And you better talk to them!' I kick him in the shin. That only hurts my toe so I run back down to the jetty where Saleesi will help me whomp him if he comes chasing after me. I thought maybe to cripple him so he don't run off but he jus' growls and yells for people to grab knives and hide. That young man, Tyrell Weatherman, is hiding behind a big water trough near the windmill. I'm keeping my eye on him.

Jacob sits down at the fire-pit, and jabs at it with a big iron poker sending sparks shooting up. If I were Valley of the Sun people I wouldn't be going near him.

'Girl!' Jacob yells. 'You tell them come up here and talk like regular folk!'

This was what I wanted all along. That's why I done all this.

The Valley of the Sun people is a bit quieter when they step off on this jetty and maybe Marta's given them one of her talking-tos.

'Troublesome child,' the older woman mutters at me when she steps off *Licorice*. 'Why have you dragged us out here?'

Marta heaves herself onto the jetty. 'I told you, this also concerns Jacob's Reach. That's why she wants you here.'

The older woman with the black hair instead of grey is still scowling. 'She told one of our people she had information about the murder of Gerra's sister,' she says. 'We want to hear what it is!'

'Did you say that, Neoma?' Marta asks.

I nod. 'But I said "death" not "murder".' Marta is right when she said words can be dangerous.

Marta waves up to the fire-pit. 'Then we shall hear it. Perhaps we should all sit down and take tea, as is the custom in the Ockery Islands.'

And I don't know what Marta thinks I know, coz I ain't told her. How could I without admitting I been poking around out here spying on our neighbours?

'A crime has been committed and we don't have time for tea. We need the girl to tell us what she knows,' the woman says.

'The crime will have been committed whether you beat the child until she talks or whether you stop for tea, and hear her talk willingly. Which will it be?' Marta says, and I don't much like the idea of Marta suggesting I get beat till I talk!

I open my mouth to complain but Marta holds a finger up to my face. 'Not a word, until they agree to be reasonable.'

Saleesi plants herself in front of me, waving her big pirate cutlass around. 'Want me to whomp them for ya?' she asks.

The Valley of the Sun people pull out guns and point them at Saleesi.

'There's no whomping going on here!' Marta says, making Saleesi back down quick. 'By anyone!' Marta gives the people with the guns a hard look.

The older Valley of the Sun woman nods. 'Very well then,' she says. 'Tea.' But like she still don't really have time for tea.

'Come and meet Jacob,' Marta says like she can't see him sitting there fuming with a fire-poker in his hand. 'You bring the others up when they arrive,' she says to me. The little white sail of Marta's boat is still a way off. 'And then we'll hear from you.'

GERRA'S GHOST

Saleesi and I are left standing on the jetty watching as Jacob stands and shakes their hands and they all sit down while he makes tea.

Up beside one of the huts Echo is waving at me. He points at his chest and shakes his head. 'What's he doing?' I ask.

'He don't want anyone to know he tol' you anything,' Saleesi says.

I give Echo a thumbs up and he disappears back behind the hut.

When Marta's boat gets close, Ma's too busy dropping sails to give me dark looks but Gerra is sitting in the boat with her walking stick held firm in front of her, looking right at me, like . . . I dunno. Is she angry? Has she remembered what happened now? Is she angry I made her come back to this place?

I don't wait for Ma to get off before I set off up to the fire-pit, coz I don't want for Ma to grab me and give me one of them angry whispering talking-tos. I tell Saleesi to help Gerra, and for the rest of them to follow me.

Jacob's eyes go wide when he sees Gerra limping along behind me. Sweat beads on his forehead, his skin goes pale, and he drags his eyes off her and back to the dirt. I reckon he put her in a boat thinking she was dead, and now he maybe thinks her ghost has come back to make him pay.

Marta makes all the Valley of the Sun people sit down with me and Ma and Jag and his da, and then while Jacob serves them tea, his hand shaking as he fills Gerra's cup, Marta asks all sorts of questions about their intentions for the Ockery Islands.

I quietly drag the fire-poker away and stuff it hard against the log I'm sitting on. There's an axe in the woodpile nearby that's making me worried in case Jacob or Tyrell go to grab it.

We find out that Valley of the Sun are now the law

here. Our government has given up on keeping us at all after years of not being able to help us. Jus' given us away to a whole new nation!

The red flashing light tech lets them track movements of ships in the area and send messages. 'You don't know what's out there to the north,' the old woman says. 'Armies of people who prefer to take rather than build. If they come here, you'll be pleased for the protection of the Valley of the Sun.'

'And what do you get by collecting and protecting ramshackle islands that no one else wants?' Marta asks.

'The most valuable of all commodities, land for growing things,' the old woman says.

'Well, we use as much land as we dare for growing things already, so why would you protect us?' Jag's da asks.

'These islands hold the mouth to the inland sea and those larger land masses we need,' the woman says. 'You are our eyes and ears. We hope to grow food inland and ship it out past your islands.'

Marta nods slowly. 'If these technologies allow you to communicate, then can we use them to communicate? I'd like to be able to talk to the other Ockery Islands now and then.'

'No!' Jacob says. 'We live without technology!'

Marta sighs. 'We live gentle lives, now what can be more gentle than being able to let you know if we have too many bananas or dried fish and to share our resources?' she asks.

Jacob jus' says, 'Humpf!' and goes back to staring at the dirt.

'I think we can spare some handsets set on a local channel.' The older woman lifts her cup. 'Now we all have tea, can we get to the business we came here for?'

Marta waves her hand at all of us sitting stiffly on our seats, hot mugs of tea in our hands that we ain't even drinking coz we's all too worried, and says, 'This is how you approach a village in this area. You come, you bring gifts, you sit, you drink tea. Now, if you intend to be the governing law here, I trust that you will learn our ways and be patient and just with us as we learn yours. It's been a long time since anyone has had to answer to the law here. We've had to make our own.'

'You expect me to have tea with every island?' the old woman asks. 'It'll take days!'

Marta nods. 'It will take days, possibly weeks.' And she smiles politely. 'Now, what's your name?'

'Leonor.'

'Welcome to the Ockery Islands, Leonor. We live gentle lives. We live polite lives. We do not want war or raiders to come to these islands, so we will keep your technology on our hill, and help you watch this opening to the inland sea. Drink your tea,' Marta says like she's talking to someone who never met tea before.

Leonor gulps down the tea like she's surprised Marta's telling her what to do. I'm not surprised, Marta's always telling me what to do.

Marta asks Gerra if she remembers coming here before.

'She was never here!' Jacob says, but he still won't look directly at Gerra. He jus' wipes sweat from his forehead and stares at the fire.

Marta ignores him, and carries on speaking to Leonor. 'We know that Gerra and her siblings came here, but the people of Jacob's Reach dislike and fear all technology and want to live gentle lives as do all the people of the Ockery Islands, and so walking in without a word with the intent to set up tech here was bound to cause problems. We know they visited here. We know it was covered up.'

Uncle Sorren must've told Marta about our second visit after me and Jag left.

'Marta does not speak for me!' Jacob says.

Leonor with the black instead of grey hair does a really strange thing. She takes a sip of tea and looks right at him. 'This is very nice tea,' she says. 'What kind is it?'

He don't answer. He's feeling around for where he left the poker. Maybe he's thinking he's in real big trouble.

'Mint,' Marta says. 'With a hint of ginger?' She lifts an eyebrow at Jacob to agree.

Jacob scowls, stands and walks towards the woodpile.

Leonor drops her voice. 'Who do you think we should take for questioning from Jacob's Reach?'

Marta thinks and sighs. 'I would say you should take Jacob himself, given how he keeps tight control on his people and how hot to temper he is, unless anyone else comes forward and says they did it.'

I'm standing, watching that axe, but Jacob don't reach for it. He takes a split log, and puts another on top of it.

'It wasn't Jacob,' I say. 'Well, he din't start it.' I sit back down.

Marta and Leonor both tilt their heads and wait for me to speak and it's a bit scary to have two leaders looking at me in that way, and Jacob maybe listening too, but I got to go on. 'The siblings from the Valley of the Sun were cutting down the trees they bury people under. They cut down the tree that belonged to dead Aunty

Meryn, and her son got angry,' I say. Even though I don't know for sure who Aunty Meryn's son is. It's not Echo, and it can't be Jacob, coz he's too old to have a mother buried jus' a couple of years ago.

'We came back to Jacob's Reach,' Jag says. 'On the way back from Valley of the Sun.' And he seems a bit proud to be getting up to things he shouldn't. I can see I'm gonna have to give him lessons in looking sorry afterwards.

'We saw the log with the letters in it. What happened is, the guy sibling cut down the tree and they grabbed him. Do you remember, Gerra?' I ask her. I make an M and a W with my fingers. Leonor translates and Gerra nods.

'Cutting down a tree is not a cause for murder,' Leonor says.

'There ain't no murder!' Jacob says. He's stopped behind us, armload of logs, like he don't know whether to come back to the fire-pit or run away.

'It was accidental,' I say. 'Coz then Gerra and her sister went running back to the boat to get weapons. The son, he's real mad, and he's carrying the log they made out of his mother's tree, and then he sees them coming up the jetty to hurt his people and so he runs at them, thinking to chase them back to their boat maybe, who knows? Then they fire at him, with that dart thing they shot at Uncle Sorren. And coz he's running, carrying a whole tree pole right at them, he can't stop, I guess, and he knocks them both onto the rocks in his sleep and that's how Gerra got injured.'

'These people,' Marta says. 'You have to understand they're not violent, although that boy with the log, he shouldn't've lost his temper and run at them like that.'

'They put Gerra and her sister in a boat for dead and cast them out on the tide, and probably killed their brother,' Leonor says. 'The boy didn't do that. He was asleep. So we'll need to take Jacob and the boy. Which boy do you think it is, Neoma?'

'Now, see here!' Jacob says. He drops the wood and shakes a finger at that old woman. 'This girl don't know anything.'

'Not for sure,' I say. 'But I think it's Tyrell Weatherman coz of the W in Weatherman.' There's a growl from behind the trough. 'But you see, you can't be taking both of them. They have someone to trade, coz they still have the guy sibling.'

'What?' Leonor says.

'They have him in that boarded-up shack,' I say and point up the hill.

Leonor translates to Gerra, who gasps and looks at me. I nod. Finally Gerra smiles. I'm surprised her face don't crack with the effort!

'The people of the Ockery Islands are not violent,' Marta says again. 'Your engineers broke their law, they arrested one of them. How were they to know you make the law now? We've lived through some violent times before we found peace here in the Ockerys.'

'Thank you, Marta,' Jacob says. 'Yes, it was an accident. Tyrell didn't want anyone to die, and your people were treating our hill like they owned it. We didn't know you were the new government. Think of how we felt to have them stomping round on graves up there!'

'Cutting down memorial trees is certainly not what we want,' Leonor says.

'You shouldn't be cutting down no trees. Don't you remember how the world got this way? We gotta live gentle lives,' I say.

'We have to create a clear line of sight for our technology, and fence the power sources to stop people digging them up.' Leonor looks at my burnt scalp. 'We'll trade the crime of concealment, for our engineer, and take someone to work off the debt for the death of Gerra's sister. Is this fair, in your opinion?' she asks Jacob.

'No!' I say. 'Don't you go taking someone what ain't done nothing. You take the one who done it!'

Leonor frowns like she's had enough of me butting in but Marta nods. I can't believe she's backing me up.

'All people need a sense of fairness,' she says.

Leonor agrees so Marta goes to have a quiet conversation with Jacob.

'How did you find out all this information?' Leonor asks me.

I shrug. 'By being a bit wild.'

At that moment Tyrell must figure he best be far away as possible coz he stands up from behind the trough and takes off running up the hill. 'That's Tyrell,' I say, grab the fire-poker and take off after him. He's heading for the woodpile with the axe sitting in the stump. I stop, lift the poker up behind my head and biff it through the air. It smacks Tyrell in the arm jus' as he's reaching for the axe. He pulls his hand back, turns and then runs.

Saleesi passes me with a whoop. 'I'll whomp that rascal!'

Two of the Valley of the Sun People with guns are chasing him too.

'Tyrell!' Jacob bellows.

Tyrell stops dead. I stop dead. Even Saleesi stops dead.

Jacob holds up a finger and carries on talking to Marta. Then he marches over and grabs Tyrell by the arm and drags him back down to the fire-pit.

'I din't mean for it to happen!' Tyrell yells. 'I din't even know until the next day. I was jus' angry. It was my Ma!'

'I know, son,' Jacob says. Then he turns to Leonor. 'He's quick to temper and he needs to learn not to be, but he's not a bad person. He's been real affected by this horrible accident. A chance to put things right will be good for him, but he ain't got much family and I don't want him away from them for long. He ain't quite grown, he needs to be with us.'

We all trail along as Jacob deals Leonor down to keeping Tyrell for jus' six months. She agrees too quickly prolly coz Tyrell looks like he's too much trouble and she'd rather take a nice kid like Echo or someone else.

Then Jacob tells them to go and get their engineer from the shack.

The tall brother sibling comes running from the shack, hair all messy, blinking against the sun on the horizon. Then he yells, 'Gerra!' He runs and hugs

Gerra so hard he picks her up off the ground, and she drops her stick, and sobs into his shoulder. His face is covered in tears, and he runs to each Valley of the Sun person and kisses them on the cheek and hugs them and slaps their backs like they's the ones who rescued him, then he runs back and hugs Gerra again.

Ma comes and hugs me, her strong arms around me, her warm body against mine, strong rough fingers wiping the hair off my face. Uncle Sorren hugs Jag, and everyone's back where they should be. I feel sorry for Tyrell, coz he's gotta pay for reacting badly to a thing that he had no control over.

A WHOLE WORLD
OF SURPRISE

Leonor starts to walk to the jetty as if she's going but turns to me. 'Your debt has been paid,' she says. 'Please do not come sneaking around Valley of the Sun to steal people again, especially bringing those trained beasts of yours!'

'Trained beasts?' Marta asks.

I shrug. I ain't gonna admit in front of this woman that I ain't got dangerous sea creatures what can whomp her if she bothers us again.

'This child has run wild with wild animals,' Leonor says to Marta like she's telling tales on me.

Marta smiles too politely. The kind of smile us kids

know to run away from. 'Our children are our greatest asset,' she says.

Me, I'm burning hot. I ain't got any politeness left in me. 'You call me wild, and you'll go back to Valley of the Sun and treat your old people and your poor people like fish offal, jus' tossed out like you don't want them!' I say.

'We do not! We have the best of everything there!' Leonor says and gets all huffy.

'Then please feed Susan,' I say. 'She worked for you until her fingers curled. She worked like a slave barely earning a thing and you leave her to starve and sleep on the stairs.'

'Don't you have a heart?' Jag says, and stands up beside me. And coz we're standing, eyeing off this boss woman, Saleesi comes and stands next to us too. All of us side by side against the Valley of the Sun.

The woman looks me up and down. This woman who told me I'm too wild. A wild spark. No end of trouble. This woman who stole my best friend to teach me a lesson. I give her Ma's thunderhead eyes and say, 'You call me wild, but we don't treat anyone in our village that way.'

Marta steps up beside us too. 'Is this true? You don't care for the weakest among you? You run slaves? Is that the kind of society you're bringing to the Ockery Islands?'

'Slaves?' Jacob asks, and he's hanging onto Tyrell like he's changed his mind.

The woman looks from Marta to me. 'They are usually paid something. Sometimes not enough, but something. You have to understand, the Valley of the Sun has many people and many industries and there's not always room for everyone to live nicely. Or for us to know what every industry is doing.'

Marta sighs. 'You know, we don't use money here on the Ockery Islands. We barter and trade, but we don't keep count on the value of a human life either. We work until we can't and we are cared for by those who can. Our strength comes from all of us working together.'

Jag hurries to Gerra, where she's standing with her arms around her brother. 'You, Gerra, you feed Susan,' Jag says. 'She was an engineer like you. She was your family.'

Leonor translates.

Gerra looks from Jag to me, and finally nods.

Leonor sighs. Her huffy shoulders relax. 'Perhaps there are things we can teach each other,' she says. 'I hope you don't mind if I call on you for tea again.'

Marta nods. 'That would be wonderful. Go gently.'

They shake hands.

Jacob walks Tyrell to the jetty with his arm around his shoulders, and Echo runs down from one of the houses with a bag for Tyrell to take.

We watch them sail away in their tin boat with the gold sun on the bow.

'Looks like we got some law around here now,' Marta says slowly. 'I'm not sure where they came from, but it's probably a good idea.'

'They come from a floating island made out of mega ships stuck together,' I say. 'And slung between them is this massive garden valley growing crops.'

Marta laughs. 'A floating island made of ships! Honestly, Neoma.'

'Honestly,' I say. 'Ask Jag.' And then I laugh too, coz Marta's got a whole world of surprise coming her way.

ALL THREE OF US

Saleesi is already too tall to stay in Rusty Bus with the other kids, her feet sticking way out into the aisle, so everyone gets busy building her a shack.

We use the top of a car for her roof so she's got a dome roof and roof windows. She can stand on a chair and look out, or wind the windows down to let the heat out with handles Uncle Sorren has made from scrap metal. The walls is a frame of wood with panels of car metal hammered around, and there's a nice cool brick floor. It's not big, but big enough for a bed and a chair which come from salvage, and another car door to enter and leave by. Ma says maybe they'll extend it and I can move in there with her too one day coz of how I have a 'calming influence' on Saleesi. Mainly coz she carries that big cutlass everywhere, and if anyone crosses her she says she's gonna whomp them. She's mostly kidding, I think.

Uncle Sorren pulls the Valley of the Sun boat out from its hiding place up the creek and we take off the golden sun and tidy it up and name it *Fish Whomper*. Saleesi says it's her salvage and the Valley of the Sun will have to fight her for it, but Marta called them on her new handset and they said we could add it to our fishing fleet for the price of a crew meal next time they's passing. Me and Jag teach Saleesi all we know about making lures and fishing on the inland sea, and how to avoid snags, and specially about cooking fish before you eat them.

Jag learned a lot working on Valley of the Sun pulling things to bits. He uses the power source to hook up Marta's old cottage and get her electric lights working again like years ago before the risen sea. We don't think it's illegal, but Marta says she'll mention it next time the Valley of the Sun comes to tea.

None of us really want to go beyond the surf coast towers again, knowing what we do about crocs that leap on boats, giant sharks and maybe a very mad pirate woman still sailing around looking for us. Saleesi says nothing can kill that old pirate hag and I believe her.

Right now, we're all perfectly happy being the best fisher team and best salvage team on the whole of the inland sea. All three of us.

ACKNOWLEDGEMENTS

What a year we are going through. Although we're only three months into 2020 as I write this, it feels like we've lived a thousand years of fires and disease. No matter how it turns out, it will be a year of lessons. Thank you to those who've reached out and supported others. We really are all in this together and acts of kindness will get us through.

Thank you to everyone at Allen & Unwin, especially Susannah Chambers for your constant encouragement, and to Jodie Webster and Hilary Reynolds for taking on the challenge of bringing this book into the world. It's been lovely working with you. Thanks too to Jo Hunt for coming on this three-book journey with me and designing the amazing covers that invite readers in. I've loved all of them.

ABOUT THE AUTHOR

Multi award-winning Australian author Bren MacDibble was raised on farms all over New Zealand, but moved to Australia as an adult. After twenty years in Melbourne, her house was destroyed in a fire. Bren restored the house, then sold it and her remaining possessions and spent the next two years living and working in a bus travelling around Australia. She currently lives on the west coast. She has written educational stories and taught creative writing for many years. *Across the Risen Sea* is the latest title in an environmentally-themed middle-grade series inspired by her observations on her travels.

Also by Bren MacDibble: H O W   T O   B E E

Winner, Children's Book Council Australia
Best Book for Younger Readers, 2018
Winner, 2018 New Zealand Children's Book of the Year,
Esther Glen Award for Junior Fiction

Nine year-old Peony lives in a shack in the orchard and dreams of becoming the best 'bee' the farm has ever seen, scrambling through the fruit trees to pollinate by hand with feather wands. She has love, she has enough to eat and if she could just become a 'bee' she'd be super-cherries happy. But her mother wants her to live in the city, where all the fruit is sent. Torn between two different worlds, Peony fights to protect her family and the world she loves.

'This powerful, engrossing and engaging novel is a great introduction to dystopian fiction and tackles environmental issues, poverty, social inequality and problematic family relationships. Peony is a strong and inspiring protagonist and, despite some of the darker themes, this is a story filled with hope, as unlikely friendships blossom and a strong sense of loyalty prevails.' - Seven Stories, The National Centre for Children's Books

'Quirky, original and heartfelt, this is an all too plausible dystopian adventure, exploring themes of family loyalty and the environment.' - Fiona Noble, The Bookseller

'How to Bee is a moving, intelligent novel, offering plenty of food for thought and a cast of appealing - and not so appealing - characters which linger with you long after the story is finished...' - North Somerset Teachers' Book Award

Also by Bren MacDibble: THE DOG RUNNER

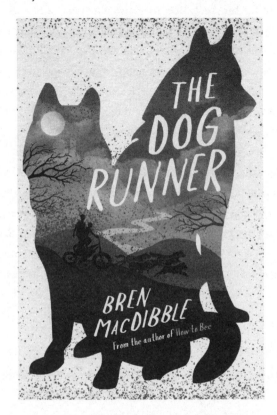

Nominated for the CILIP Carnegie Award 2020
Shortlisted for the Hearst Group Red Magazine
Book of the Year Award 2019
Shortlisted, Children's Book Council Australia
Best Book for Younger Readers, 2020
Winner, 2019 New Zealand Children's Book of the Year,
Esther Glen Award for Junior Fiction

Ella and her brother, Emery, are alone in a city that's starving to death. If they are going to survive, they must get away, up-country, to find Emery's mum. But how can two kids travel such big distances across a dry, barren and dangerous landscape? Well, when you've got five big doggos and a dry-land dogsled, the answer is you go mushing. But when Emery is injured, Ella must find a way to navigate them through rough terrain, and even rougher encounters with desperate people.

Other fiction titles by Australian authors available from Old Barn Books:

The Stars at Oktober Bend, by Glenda Millard
Shortlisted for the CILIP Carnegie Medal 2017

Alice Nightingale if fifteen, with hair as red as fire and skin as pale as bone, but something inside her is broken. Manny James runs at night, trying to escape his memories. He sees Alice on the roof of her river-house, looking like a figurehead on a ship sailing through the stars. He has a poem in his pocket and he knows the words by heart. He is sure that girl has written them.

> *'Surprising, lyrical and beautiful, this book speaks of hope in the darkest of times, and of love in its many forms. The voices of Alice and Manny are distinctive and memorable, and their resilience will stay with me…'* Liz Flanagan, author of Eden Summer

A Small Free Kiss in the Dark, by Glenda Millard

Skip's an outsider, a quiet observer. He draws pictures to make sense of the world. He's never fitted in. So he takes to the streets. Life there may be hard, but it's better than the one he's left behind, especially when he teams up with old Billy. Then come the bombs which leave little Max in his care, and also Tia, the sad dancer, with her sweet baby, Sixpence. Scavenging for food, sheltering in an empty funfair, living on love and imagination… how long can Skip's fragile new family hold out as war grips the city?

A Different Dog, by Paul Jennings

The forest is dense and dark. And the trail full of unexpected perils. The dog can't move. The boy can't talk. And you won't know why. Or where you are going. You will put this story down to not wanting the journey to end. But it's from Paul Jennings so watch out for the ambush.

A Different Boy, by Paul Jennings
Longlisted for the CILIP Carnegie Medal 2019

The orphanage is far behind. But life as a stowaway is even worse. And nothing is what it seems on this sea of troubles. Will Anton survive? Can you guess the shocking truth? Another compelling tale from the master storyteller.

A Different Land, by Paul Jennings
Nominated for the CILIP Carnegie Medal

Christopher is twelve thousand miles from home. The pub has a dirt floor and the owner is as rough as guts. The forest hides snakes, feral pigs and a dark secret. Mysterious, bold and strange. Expect the unexpected. And watch your step.
Enter this place and you will be different for ever.